Confused, Ian watched Mimi leave, his eyes lingering on her swaying hips

His mouth grew dry. Her legs, bared in a short skirt, were luscious, and he could imagine them wrapped around his waist as he—

Suddenly, she turned around and walked back to him. Ian braced himself, hands shoved firmly in his pockets. She put her hands on his shoulders and kissed his cheek. The caress was there and gone before his brain realized it had happened.

"Thank you for being so wonderful with my son."

She turned and walked away again. This time she didn't look back. Ian followed her with his eyes all the way up the street until she disappeared. He felt light-headed and sluggish, as if someone had slipped him a drug. He was getting in too deep, he told himself, yet he couldn't convince himself to heed the warning. The depths that threatened to drown him looked too inviting.

Dear Reader,

From the moment Ian Berzani appeared on the page, he fascinated me. He is the calm center in the volatile Berzani family: unflappable, careful and considerate. But what is going on inside this quiet, strong man? What dreams, desires, wants and needs does he have?

I knew I had to write Ian's story. I had to know if he could reach for his own brass ring while remaining true to his heart. In the end, Ian surprised even me. I hope you will enjoy his journey as much as I did.

Please visit me at www.lisaruff.net. And keep a watch out for my next book from Harlequin.

Happy reading,

Lisa Ruff

An Unexpected Father

LISA RUFF

HARLEQUIN®

TORONTO • NEW YORK • LONDON
AMSTERDAM • PARIS • SYDNEY • HAMBURG
STOCKHOLM • ATHENS • TOKYO • MILAN • MADRID
PRAGUE • WARSAW • BUDAPEST • AUCKLAND

Recycling programs
for this product may
not exist in your area.

ISBN-13: 978-0-373-75307-9

AN UNEXPECTED FATHER

ABOUT THE AUTHOR

Lisa Ruff was born in Montana and grew up in Idaho but met the man of her dreams in Seattle. She married Kirk promising to love, honor and edit his rough drafts. His pursuit of writing led Lisa to the craft. A longtime reader of romance, she decided to try to create one herself. The first version of *Man of the Year* took three months to finish, but her day job got in the way of polishing the manuscript. She stuffed it in a drawer where it languished for several years.

In pursuit of time to write and freedom to explore the world, Lisa, Kirk and their cat sailed from Seattle on a 37-foot boat. They spent five years cruising in Central America and the Caribbean. Lisa wrote romance, but it took a backseat to an adventurous life. She was busy writing travel essays, learning to speak Spanish from taxi drivers and handling a small boat in gale-force winds.

When she returned to land-life, she finally revised *Man of the Year* and sent it to an agent. Within a year, she had a contract from Harlequin American Romance.

She and her husband are cruising on a sailboat again somewhere in the Atlantic Ocean. When not setting sail for another port, she is working on her next Harlequin romance book.

Books by Lisa Ruff

HARLEQUIN AMERICAN ROMANCE

1214—MAN OF THE YEAR
1243—BABY ON BOARD

For Ethan and Graham,
sons of sailors, both

Chapter One

Ian shut the wood-shop door behind him. A warm breeze brushed his face and he automatically looked up at the flag over the marina office. *West by Northwest*. Even though the sky was dark with the threat of rain, the wind was perfect for sailing south. He could be in Norfolk by noon tomorrow. He wouldn't stop, though. He would just hang a left at the mouth of the Chesapeake and head out to sea, straight for Bermuda.

The longing for freedom, for the wind and endless expanse of open sea, was so strong, Ian ached with the possibility.

Sighing, he walked across the boatyard. He wasn't going anywhere, not today. Today, he was going to go finish the teak trim on Buckman's boat so the varnishers could start coating the wood. Then he would go on to the next project and the one after that. Four months. Then he could leave. Ian stepped onto the ramp that connected the dock to the shore. Lost in his reverie, he almost missed seeing the young boy who was crouched down at the water's edge. He was poking a stick at a clump of reeds in the rocks.

"Hey, kid. Leave that alone. That might be a duck's nest in there."

The boy looked up and slowly stood. "I wasn't doing nothing."

"*Anything*," Ian said, then winced. Since when had he become a grammarian?

"Whatever. You sound like my mother."

Ian had to laugh. The kid had hit the mark, dead-on. He took a better look at him. Though he tried to sound tough, the boy was small and scrawny. He was dressed in faded jeans that had both knees blown out. A black, hooded sweatshirt covered a white T-shirt and hung down past his hips, dwarfing his thin frame. Except for the holes in the jeans and the bagginess of the clothes, Ian was dressed the same, right down to the color of the hoodie.

"You and I must go to the same tailor," Ian said with a smile.

The kid just stared back at him silently. Sandy-brown hair mingled with brows the same color and partially covered eyes that were a deep, intense blue. Those eyes were full of sullen antipathy. Ian didn't take the hostility personally. It looked as if the kid's face was permanently set in that grumpy mold.

"Your parents have a boat in the yard?" Ian asked.

"No."

"Do they moor one here?"

"No."

Ian sighed. "Then what are you doing hanging around?"

The boy shrugged and lowered his lashes. He dug the end of the stick he still carried into the mud at his feet. His black-and-white tennis shoes were liberally coated with the same muck, as if he had been poking around the shoreline for a while. With another sigh—this one in exasperation—Ian stuck his hands into the pockets of his sweatshirt.

"This isn't a playground, kid. It's kind of dangerous."

The boy looked up at him and rolled his eyes. "Yeah, right."

Ian pointed toward the gate at the back of the boatyard. "Scram."

"You can't tell me what to do," the kid said. "You're not my dad."

"No, but I could be."

The kid rolled his eyes again and snorted. "You don't own the world."

"Nope." Ian cocked his head. "But I own this little corner of it."

"Do not."

"Do, too." Ian shook his head. He was supposed to be the adult here, he reminded himself. He tried again. "What's your name?"

"My mom told me not to talk to strangers."

"She tell you not to trespass, too? Where do you live?"

"None of your business."

"I'm making it my business." Ian took a step closer.

The boy dropped the stick and turned around, poised to run. Ian reached out a hand and snagged the hood of the sweatshirt, stopping the flight before it started. "Hold on there, kid. You're not going anywhere."

"Lemme go!" The boy shrugged and tried to squirm away.

Ian dropped a hand on the kid's shoulder and turned him around. He was done putting up with the little smart-ass. "Where's home, kid?" he asked firmly.

For a minute, the boy looked as if he was going to balk, then he jerked his head to the left. "My grandpop owns the Laughing Gull. That's where I live. So lemme go."

"George is your grandfather?" Ian knew the owner of the local bar, but never realized he had a grandson. He spun the kid back around and began to propel him forward.

"Well, let's go talk to your grandfather then. Maybe he can answer my questions."

The boy shot him an angry glance, his mouth set in a mulish line of stubbornness. Ian ignored it and kept his grip firm on the kid's shoulder. With all the work he had to do, this was one more interruption he didn't need. At this rate he wouldn't get anything else done today and then the yard would be another day behind schedule.

MIMI HELD THE PHONE to her ear, listening to the ring on the other end of the connection and biting her lip. *No answer.* When the voice mail came on, she said, "Hi. It's Mom. Where are you? School's been out for an hour. Grandmom and Grandpop are still gone, so I'm here at the bar." She paused, then added, "I'm worried, so call me soon, Jacky."

She closed the cell phone and slipped it into her back pocket. Where could he be? It was already three-fifteen. She went to the tables by the side windows, looking out to see if Jack was coming up the road. A couple of cars drove by, but there was no sign of her son.

The Laughing Gull, the waterside bar her parents had owned for over thirty years, was quiet—typical for mid-afternoon on a Tuesday. Her last customers had been a couple who drank a quick beer, hunched over a collection of brochures they spread out on the table. She supposed they were shopping for a new boat, judging by the photos she saw when she delivered their drinks. After they left, not another soul passed through the door. It would be busy later, the place filling with workers from the nearby marinas. Locals would filter in after that for an evening drink or a quick snack.

Mimi ignored the empty glasses on the table and wandered to the windows at the back of the room. Although the

Laughing Gull fronted a busy street, it had mostly turned its back to the traffic and commotion, preferring the more pleasant and tranquil view of Crab Creek. Instead of windows, the entrance and the bar stretched across the front wall with a small kitchen tucked behind them. To the left side of that, a second, smaller door opened out onto a patio that was seldom used. The rest of the walls were mostly window from table height up to the ceiling to take advantage of the view.

Standing between two tables, Mimi gazed out on Crab Creek rippling and flowing right past the Gull's back windows. Her parents' house—the house she had grown up in—was nestled behind a bank of lush, green viburnum on the left; to the right, A&E Marine's silver-gray sheds and docks full of boats. Opposite the Gull, the shore curved away, opening at the mouth of the inlet. The bend gave the bar's back windows a view out onto the Chesapeake Bay itself. Mimi had grown up with the view and only now, after ten years' absence, did she appreciate the panorama. Everywhere else along the creek, houses had sprouted on top of houses to catch even the smallest glimpse of the water.

Before her parents bought it, the Laughing Gull had been a seedy, smoke-filled dive that catered to local watermen and workers at a nearby cannery. The beams that crisscrossed the white ceiling were rumored to have come from the *Cosmonaut,* a ship that sank near Thomas Point Light. The oak floors had been scavenged from a dance hall that had partially burned down in the forties. Her father had refinished the planks, but under the polish and gleam, they still bore the scars and blemishes from decades of fox-trots, waltzes and two-steps.

Mimi sighed and turned away from the view. Picking up the glasses left by her last customers, she took them behind the bar to the sink. It *was* comforting to be back home, even if she had tucked her tail and run to get here. Ten years. Wasted. She washed the glasses and set them on the drain board, then slipped a new CD into the stereo and turned up the volume.

Halfway through the second song, Mimi checked the time on her cell phone and wondered about Jack again. Her parents should be home soon and then she could chase him down. She hoped he had just made a new friend and was having too much fun to answer the call. Or they were playing a video game, and didn't hear the phone. The normal, happy things kids did. Mimi doubted either of those events had occurred. Jack didn't *do* normal and happy these days. Picking up a rag, she wiped the already-clean bar top again. The bangles on her wrist clanged together and clacked on the wood as she rubbed the smooth oak surface. She wished someone would come in to distract her. Anyone. A friendly face and an order to serve would be a welcome diversion.

Two songs later, as if in answer to her thought, the front door of the bar opened and her son walked inside.

Mimi smiled widely. "Hey, kiddo! I've been wondering where you—"

The rest of her greeting died in her throat as a stranger followed Jack inside. The man towered over her son. His dark curling hair framed an angular and striking face, with an aquiline nose over lips that Mimi instantly—embarrassingly—imagined kissing. She wrenched her gaze from his mouth only to collide with dark brown eyes. They held hers for a long moment, sending her a message she couldn't interpret, before she finally got the strength to look away. Her gaze traveled down his long, lean body instead, which did nothing to restore her voice.

She almost laughed when she saw that he was dressed exactly like her son, but on this man, the clothes actually fit. *Really* fit. Broad shoulders filled out the sweatshirt; the white cotton of his T-shirt stretched across a muscled chest. The faded denims he wore clung in all the right spots. Mimi closed her eyes for a second. When she looked at him again, a smile flitted across his face. There and gone so quickly, she wasn't sure if she had imagined it.

"I don't have to ask if you're related to this boy," the man said in a quiet baritone.

People often said she and Jack looked alike, which pleased Mimi. They shared the same hair color: sandy-brown mixed with lighter gold giving it a slightly sun-streaked look. Their eyes were the same blue, too. But Mimi saw more of Jack's father in the shape of his face. Jack had a squarer jaw, and his high cheekbones were gaining definition as he streaked toward puberty.

Jack climbed onto one of the stools and threw a glare at the man. "I wasn't doing nothing, I—"

"*Any*thing," Mimi corrected absently. Taking a deep breath, she released her grip on the rag she had unconsciously twisted tightly. She dropped it in the sink and dried off her hands. Turning down the stereo a touch, she walked from behind the bar and held out her hand. "Hello, I'm Mimi Green, Jack's mother."

"So that's his name. Jack." He slanted a glance at the boy, then looked back at Mimi. "Ian Berzani."

Her hand was enfolded in a warm, callused grip, shaken once and released. Her palm tingled from the contact. Ian put his hands in his pockets, but offered no other words. Closer to him now, Mimi caught a faint whiff of new-cut wood, crisp and tangy. A few chips of it flecked his hair and she itched to brush them away. She stuck her hands into the back pockets of her jeans, keeping herself from acting on the impulse.

"Is Anna Berzani your sister?" she asked, making small talk to cover her agitation.

Ian nodded once, still taciturn.

"We were at school together," Mimi said. "A long time ago."

"Mmm."

She laughed a little, uncomfortable with his reserve. He said nothing to help her move the conversation. "Is she around?" she tried again.

"No. She's lived on the West Coast for years."

Mimi smiled at the information. Anna had always said she was out of Crab Creek as soon as the ink was dry on her diploma. It was a goal they had shared that deepened their friendship all those years ago. "Well, tell her I said hello when you talk to her."

"You can tell her yourself. She's coming for a visit on Friday."

"Really?" This was exciting news. "I'd love to see her!"

He nodded again. They stood in awkward silence, tension humming between them for a long moment, until Jack interrupted impatiently.

"Mom, tell him to get lost. I wasn't doing—"

"You always order adults around like that, kid?" Ian asked. One dark eyebrow lifted as he looked at the boy through slightly narrowed eyes.

Mimi flushed as if the rebuke had been aimed at her. "Jack! Apologize for being so rude."

Jack stuck out his lower lip and glowered at them both. Mimi's lips tightened in impatience. She had been the recipient of that sullen stare too often over the past few weeks. The man at her side shook his head and her embarrassment deepened.

"Be careful, kid," Ian said, his eyes flickering back and

forth between her and Jack. "Your face is going to get stuck like that."

"I'm sorry," Mimi said, turning to face Ian. "Has he done something wrong?"

"Trespassing," Ian said flatly. "And generally being a smart-ass." The dark eyes surveyed the boy for a moment. "The first charge can be overlooked, but I'm not so sure about the second."

"Trespassing! Where?"

"In the yard." Ian jerked his head in the direction of the masts and buildings of the marina visible through the window.

"Did he do any damage? I'll be glad to—"

"No," Ian said, interrupting her apology. "He just shouldn't play there. It's too dangerous."

Mimi stiffened, finding a criticism of her parenting hidden in his words. "Yes, I suppose it could be," she said tartly. "If I'd known, I wouldn't have let him go there."

"No, you probably wouldn't."

There was no inflection in the statement, but her hackles rose anyway. "What's that supposed to mean?"

Ian tilted his head to one side slightly. His dark eyes narrowed again. "What do you think it means?"

"I can look after my child."

"Did I say you couldn't?"

"Look, Mr. Berzani—"

"Mr. Berzani is my dad." A frown dipped the man's eyebrows in disapproval. "Call me Ian."

The frown made Mimi flush again. She struggled to control herself. Why was she reacting this way? Why was everything he said a challenge? She wasn't usually so edgy, but something about Ian Berzani made her lose her usual poise.

Looking up into his handsome face, Mimi tried to read

his expression, but there was nothing there to grasp. Unlike the musicians with whom she had spent the past ten years, this man gave none of his feelings away. His face—his eyes—were impassive. There was no boundless energy giving way to wild, wide gestures. He simply stood; distant, aloof and unapproachable.

"Can I go now?" Jack said, interrupting Mimi's thoughts.

"Not until you apologize to Mr. Berzani."

The boy huffed a sigh through his nose. "*Sorry.*"

"Wow," Ian said, both eyebrows raised as he looked down at Jack. "I can feel the agony and remorse from here."

The dry sarcasm in Ian's voice made Mimi want to laugh. Jack ducked his head, but Mimi saw the grin he was trying to hide, too. Ian had obviously dealt with young boys before. Her humor didn't assuage her irritation, though. Her son was getting the upper hand.

"Jack, don't be—"

Her exasperated words were cut off as the door to the bar swung open. Mimi's parents stepped inside, their faces bright with laughter. Jack spun on his stool and faced his grandparents after shooting her a look of triumph. Mimi knew he would use them to end the interrogation. Ian looked over at her and shrugged while she sighed in frustration.

"Let it ride," he advised.

Mimi frowned. Later, in private, she would take the issue up with her son again.

"Hey, you two," she said with a lightness she didn't feel. "It's about time you showed up."

"We decided to go for a walk after lunch," her father said, dropping a kiss on her cheek. "And since we were out, we did a few errands. Thought we'd take advantage of the freedom you've given us."

Mimi slipped an arm around him. "Anytime, old man."

"Old? Who are you calling old?" He looked down at her with a scowl. His blue eyes held a smile. He squeezed her to his side and held out a hand to Ian. "Sneaking in for a drink during the workday again, Ian?" he asked, eyes twinkling.

The two men gripped hands. "George," Ian said, his face lighting briefly with that same smile Mimi imagined she had seen earlier. "I don't have much to do this time of year, so I thought I'd blow an hour or two here."

His tone was dry and her father chuckled. "Well, it's nice to see you. It's been a while since you've come by."

"Not enough hours in the day," Ian said with a shrug. "I'm usually beat by the end of it."

Claire Green patted his arm. She looked trim and pretty in her pink sweater, her blond hair immaculately coiffed. "How are you, Ian?"

"I'm fine. It's good to see you," he said, brushing a kiss across her cheek.

"I saw your mother last week at the post office. She is so thrilled with that new grandbaby of hers," Claire said with a smile.

Ian laughed. "That's an understatement. She's addicted to the baby. Lucky for her, Patrick brings Beth with him to the yard most days, so she can get her fix."

"He dotes on that child, doesn't he?"

"You'd think he was competing for Father of the Year or something."

Mimi watched the exchange without a word. The easy affection between her parents and this enigmatic man puzzled her. How could he be so warm and open with them, but so taciturn with her?

"You two catching up on old times?" Claire asked Mimi.

Mimi frowned, shaking her head. "We've never met before, have we?" she asked Ian. She knew they hadn't. She definitely would have remembered *him*.

"Nope."

"I'm surprised," Claire said. "Mimi and Anna were inseparable those last two years of high school. She spent as much time at your parents' house as she did at home."

Ian shrugged. "Annie's the baby. The rest of us were gone by the time she was that age. I don't think anyone made it to her graduation but Ma and Pop," he added with a grin at Claire. "She's still mad about that one."

Claire and George both chuckled. Jack spun himself around on the bar stool, obviously bored by the proceedings. The clunking of his shoes on the metal base of the stool drew everyone's attention. Turning to his grandson, George put a large hand on the boy's shoulder.

"What are you doing sitting at the bar, young man?"

Jack grinned, and the change was dramatic. Mimi smiled involuntarily at the sight. Happiness had appeared so rarely on his face the past few weeks, she wanted to drink it in like an antidote against the pouts and scowls and tears that she usually saw.

"I'm trying to get some service in this gin joint," Jack said in a gruff tone. He banged a fist on the bar top and squinted at his grandfather.

George scowled. "Get off of that bar stool, mister. We don't serve your kind in this establishment."

Trying not to smile and failing, Jack thumped his fist down once again. "Discrimination, that's what it is. Why, I oughta sue—"

George scooped Jack up and off the stool, holding him

firmly under one arm. "Excuse me," he said over Jack's giggles of laughter. "I have to take out the trash."

He carried Jack toward the door, tickling him as he went. Mimi laughed at their antics, glad that Jack didn't foist his bad humor onto his grandparents. Claire was laughing, too, clapping her hands together in delight.

Mimi glanced up at Ian and found him watching her. A fire burned in the dark depths of his eyes. His face was set in stern lines of anger or pain. She couldn't tell which. She just sensed an inner turmoil. Her smile slowly faded and she bit her lower lip, uncertain if she should ask this stranger what was wrong. Ian's gaze dropped to her mouth and a muscle in his jaw twitched once, then twice. His head dipped a fraction toward hers, then turned away as Jack let out a particularly piercing squeal of laughter.

"I have to get back to work," he said, his voice low and deep. He took a step away from Mimi, now avoiding her gaze.

Mimi nodded, unable to speak. She rubbed her palms up and down her bare arms, trying to calm the spate of shivers racing across her skin.

Claire smiled over at Ian. "It was nice to see you. Say hello to your parents for me."

"I'll do that." Ian clapped Mimi's father on the shoulder. "See you later, George," he said and was out the door before anything more could be added.

Her father dropped Jack back to his feet. "Enough," he said with a whoosh of breath. "You're getting too big for me. Or I'm getting too old."

Jack laughed. "I thought you said you weren't old."

"So I lied. Let's go find something to eat."

Mimi was still staring at the door Ian had disappeared through, as if transfixed. What had just happened? Had he been about to *kiss* her?

"He's a nice boy," her mother said.

"What?"

"Ian." Claire's eyes twinkled. "And handsome, too. You must have noticed."

Mimi felt a blush creep up her cheeks. "Um, I guess so."

Her mother smiled. "He's single, I think. I'll have to ask Elaine."

"No! Don't do that." Mimi put up her hands, warding off Claire's words. "I'm not interested."

Claire shook her head. "Liar."

George walked out from the tiny kitchen behind the bar. "What was Ian doing here?" he asked. "I thought his folks didn't let him out of the yard until September."

Mimi welcomed her father's joking distraction. She did not want to discuss Ian Berzani with her mother—at least not right now. "He brought Jack home," she explained. "My darling son was trespassing at his marina." Mimi sighed and sat down at the closest table. "Where is the little pest?"

"Over at the house, supposedly doing his homework."

"I should go talk to him." She ran a hand through her hair. "He was really rude to Ian—Mr. Berzani." She stumbled over the name a bit, still dazed by the encounter and what to think of him.

George pulled out a chair for his wife. When she was seated, he joined them at the table. "Jack's just got a little adjusting to do. I'm sure Ian wasn't offended."

"That's not the point," Mimi said, looking over at her parents. "It's been six weeks. How much longer before Jack *adjusts?*"

"Give the boy time, Mimi," her mother said, putting a hand over hers.

"I'm *trying*. I just don't think Jack is. He hates school, he hates Crab Creek and sometimes I think he hates me."

"He doesn't hate you. He's just frustrated," Claire soothed. "So are you."

"I thought this was a good school," George said with a frown.

"It has nothing to do with *this* school, Dad," Mimi said with a sigh. "It's *any* school. He's just barely passing most of his classes."

"That bad, huh?" George shook his head and chuckled. "Still, the boy comes by it honestly."

Mimi frowned at her father. "I wasn't that bad of a student. I got A's in English."

"And nearly failed math and biology." George shook his head at her, his lips twisted into the wry grin she knew so well. "I signed the report cards. Remember?"

Mimi laughed. "Okay, so I wasn't the best student."

"Best! You weren't even a *good* student, Mim. But you were a good kid," he added with a smile. "Jack's a good kid, too. He's doing better, I think."

"In less than two weeks, school will be over and we'll have the summer to get him settled," Claire said. "Maybe you should look into a soccer team for him to join. Or Nancy White's grandson plays lacrosse. I know he enjoys it."

"If he would show interest in sports—in *any*thing—I would," Mimi said. She put her head in her hands, her elbows on the table. "This is all my fault. If I hadn't kept him moving all the time, he'd be happier. He doesn't have interests like other boys do. He can tell you the order of the songs on every album the Red Hot Chili Peppers made, *and recite the lyrics,* but he can't throw a baseball to save his life."

She heard her parents laugh, and raised her head. They

were smiling at her with fond indulgence. She smiled back with a rueful twist of her lips. "Am I being too dramatic?"

Claire shook her head, her hand over her mouth, eyes dancing with humor. The door to the bar swung open and a couple walked inside. George rose to his feet. He called a greeting to the man and woman, who were regulars. Claire gazed at her daughter, sympathy lighting her pale green eyes.

"Give him time," her mother repeated. "Okay?"

Mimi frowned, but nodded. "I'll try." She rose to her feet. "I better see how he's doing."

Mimi turned and walked out of the bar. She wished she could believe her mother was right, but six weeks had not improved her son's disposition. Something was wrong, something she couldn't fix—especially if he wouldn't tell her what it was.

At times like this, Mimi wished Jack had a father, a man who could steer him through the mysteries of boyhood. Ian Berzani's face suddenly popped into her head, but she pushed the possibility away. He did not seem like the type, not after what had happened today. He seemed more interested in keeping the boy off his property and out of his sight. And he certainly wasn't interested in her, either. Mimi shook her head slowly as a shiver of memory slid across her skin.

Chapter Two

Ian rushed away from the Laughing Gull, long strides taking him to safety, without knowing exactly what danger he was fleeing. Inside the main gate of the boatyard, he hurried past rows of boats in various states of repair. Spring was rapidly becoming summer on the Chesapeake Bay, and A&E Marine was in full, frantic rush, trying to keep up with all the work. A few employees, busy patching, waxing or launching boats, waved or called a greeting to Ian, but he didn't allow anyone to slow his progress. He hurried on, letting them assume he was too busy to stop and chat.

When he reached the protection of his workshop, Ian closed the door behind him with a thump. Groaning, he leaned back against the steel panel and pulled his hands out of his pockets. They were clenched into fists, cords of muscle standing out strongly. Slowly, with effort, Ian relaxed them and studied them under the fluorescent lights. The palms were white and bloodless with red indentations where his fingernails had pressed hard into the flesh. As he stared at them, they slowly regained color.

What the hell had just happened?

Ian dropped his arms and rested his head back against the cool metal. He closed his eyes and a vision of Mimi Green's face filled his mind: thick-lashed blue eyes over a freckled nose with a lush mouth that begged to be kissed.

Unconsciously, his fingers rubbed together, as if aching to sift through the silky, sun-streaked mass of her hair. He opened his eyes to banish the image, and gazed at his worktable scattered with tools and scraps of wood. He took a deep breath, then another and another. How could a woman unnerve him so completely?

The door pushed against his back, nudging him forward. Ian stumbled away and whirled around to see his brother come through the door.

"Where have you been?" Patrick asked. "I expected to find you on Buckman's boat. You know it was supposed to be finished yesterday. I can—" He stopped and looked at Ian with a frown. "What's wrong?"

"Nothing."

Patrick's gray eyes narrowed. "Are you sick or something?"

"No." Ian turned and walked to the workbench to avoid explaining to his brother what he could not explain to himself. He opened a drawer in the tool chest and randomly grabbed a chisel. "I just came up to get this," he said, holding the tool up.

"Are you sure you're okay?"

"Yeah. Just tired. Too much work, I guess. I should be done with Buckman this afternoon." Ian moved past Patrick and yanked the door open. "Anything else?"

Patrick followed Ian out the door and fell in step with him back toward the docks. "I've almost got the boats ready for Saturday."

Ian slid a glance at his brother. "Saturday?"

"Sailing school? Remember?"

Slapping a hand to his forehead, Ian groaned. "No. I must have blocked it."

Patrick grinned. "You promised, bro."

Ian shot Patrick an irritated scowl. "I don't remember that, either."

"Come on, it'll be fun."

"Yeah, fun like having your teeth drilled without Novocain."

"It won't be that bad," Patrick said. "Besides, McKenzie's going to help out, too."

"Evan volunteered?" Ian was amazed. "I thought he was afraid of kids."

"Not kids, *babies,*" Patrick said with a laugh. "More accurately, he's afraid of one baby. Beth. I promised him that I'd leave her at home with Kate."

"What does she see in him anyway?" Ian shook his head.

"Beats me, but she completely adores him. And she doesn't care that he doesn't want anything to do with her." Patrick shrugged. "They say babies have poor vision the first few months. Maybe she'll grow out of it."

"I never thought we'd see Evan McKenzie running from a female."

Patrick's laughter joined his brother's. "So, Saturday. Ten o'clock."

"Do you *really* need me?" Ian asked. "I've got a lot to do before October."

"It's only the first week of June, Ian," Patrick said, rolling his eyes. "And haven't I been taking over a lot of your workload? Between me and that new shipwright you hired, you practically don't even *have* a job."

"As if. Pop's got some new project he wants me to look at. I've still got to build *Minerva*'s dinghy—"

"It's only for two hours," Patrick insisted. "Three, max."

"Times twelve *weeks*. That's thirty-six hours at least." Ian glared at his brother.

"I've got ten kids showing up Saturday morning to sail, Ian." Patrick crossed his arms over his chest. "You're not going to disappoint them, are you?"

Ian took a deep breath and ran a hand through his hair. His irritation had little to do with Patrick or the sailing school he had set up. His brother was just a convenient whipping boy. He *had* promised. Maybe it would even be fun.

"All right," Ian said with a sigh. "I'll be there."

"Good. I knew I could count on you." Patrick looked at him closely again, frowning. "Are you *sure* you're okay?"

"I'm fine." Ian shrugged and looked away. "I've got to get back to Buckman's project. Tell the varnishers to get ready for finish-sanding tomorrow. They should be able to get a first coat on in the afternoon."

Patrick nodded. "I'll call Buckman, too."

"Better you than me. He's not too happy the project's taken so long."

"Then he shouldn't have asked for all those extras," Patrick said with a grin. "Don't worry about it. I'll calm him down."

"Thanks." Ian turned and strode down the ramp to the pier.

"Evan and I are having a beer later," Patrick called to him. "Why don't you join us?"

"What about the wife and kid?" Ian asked, stopping and turning around.

"Kate and Molly are going over to Suzanne's tonight and taking Beth with them. That makes me a bachelor for a few hours," Patrick explained, winking.

"I've got a lot to do, Patty—"

"Come on. It's my first free night in forever and you're sloughing me off? Meet us at the Gull."

Ian hesitated. The idea of going back to the bar sent a shiver across his skin, a tightening of his nerves. "I'll pass. I'm tired of that place."

"*Tired* of it? You haven't been down there in months." Patrick shook his head and put his hands on his hips. "Come to think of it, I don't think you've been *anywhere* in months."

"You and Evan have fun."

Patrick cocked one eyebrow up. "You can't let us go out on the town alone."

The thought of how dangerous Patrick and Evan could be together did give Ian pause. Reluctantly, he nodded. "I suppose you're right."

"Good. We'll meet Evan at the Gull and go on, maybe down to the tiki bar on the Magothy River."

"All right. What time?"

"Seven."

With a wave, Ian turned and walked down the dock, worried and unsettled. The last thing he wanted was to see Mimi Green. Not before he had a chance to figure out what had happened between them. As his feet tromped on the dock, he startled a pair of mallards. They burst out of the water in a wild flapping of wings that startled Ian out of his thoughts. The birds were everywhere this time of year, engaged in their annual mating dance. The pair flew off. Ian gave himself a mental shake and climbed onto the boat.

Nothing had happened.

He had just had a momentary surge of lust for a pretty face and a tight T-shirt. He was building this up into something it wasn't. Down in the cabin, Ian picked up a piece of teak and his drill. Fitting a quarter-inch bit into the chuck, he tried to push all thoughts of her out of his head. He was leaving in four months. Nothing was going to stop him this time, especially not a woman.

Once before, he had changed plans for that reason. That woman had become more important to him than sailing around the world. For almost a year, he had shaped his future around her. One dark day, he abruptly realized that she had no interest in doing the same for him. In fact, she had no more interest in him at all. After picking up the pieces of his broken heart, Ian had decided he was going to be single-minded in pursuing his goal. No more detours. He was going to sail around the world and he was going to do it *alone*.

As he drilled through a piece of teak trim, he forced the image of blue eyes and a kissable mouth out of his head. It was lust, pure and simple. Just like the mallards in June. Mimi Green meant nothing to him. She never would. Never.

MIMI SMILED AS SHE SET BEER coasters in front of the two men. "Good evening. What can I get you guys?"

"A Yuengling," the dark-haired man said with a smile.

The silver-gray eyes weren't familiar, but his face and the smile were. "Are you a Berzani?" she asked.

The man grinned. "Guilty as charged. Patrick Berzani," he said, holding out a hand. "How did you know?"

"Are you kidding? You all look alike." The other man—blond with amazing green eyes—laughed as he spoke. He turned to Mimi. "You should have been at his wedding. It was a nightmare keeping them all straight."

"I'm Mimi Green," she said as she shook Patrick's hand. "I went to school with Anna." For some reason, she didn't want to mention meeting Ian earlier in the day.

"Hurricane Annie," the blond said with a snort of laughter. "A tempest in every teapot."

"Watch it," Patrick said, frowning. "That's my sister you're talking about."

"Like *you* haven't called her that?"

Patrick grinned and shot a glance at Mimi. "That's different."

Mimi laughed: brothers were all alike. Every one she had ever met tormented their sisters endlessly, but fought to the death if anyone else tried to do the same.

"She's coming out this weekend," Patrick said to Mimi. "I'll let her know you're around."

"Thanks, I'd appreciate that. It would be great to see her."

"Don't bet on it," the blond said with a smirk. At the same time, he held out his hand and she put hers into it. He kissed the back of it dramatically. "The one and only Evan McKenzie, at your command." He smiled up at her and winked.

"He's one of a kind, all right," Patrick said. "Good thing, too."

"It's nice to meet you both," she said with a laugh. "What can I get you?" she asked Evan.

"I'll have a summer ale and your phone number," Evan said.

Mimi laughed and turned to Patrick. "He's not *that* original."

"Hey, give me a chance here," Evan protested.

With a shake of her head, Mimi turned away. "I'll be back with your drinks."

The chuckles behind her told her they got the message. Evan would probably tease her a bit more, but neither man would be a problem, she was sure of that. Maybe it was genetic—passed on from her father—but wherever it came from, Mimi had a knack for telling which customers were going to cause trouble and which weren't.

Of course, she had spent a lot of time in bars over the years, so that might explain some of her intuition, too. Belting out songs on the stage was different than slinging drinks, but both involved reading the customer. If she judged her listeners accurately, read their reactions to the music, she could give her songs more emotional power without becoming maudlin or melodramatic. When she was in tune with her audience, it was the most intoxicating feeling in the world. She could keep them coming back for more, night after night.

With a sigh, Mimi pushed the memory to the back of her mind. Music was the past; tending bar was the present. She had given up the life of a singer partly for Jack's sake, partly because success in front of a band was so elusive. She refused to regret her choice. She had squarely faced reality—turning from her dreams and the road—and set to the task of making a stable home for herself and her son. It had been the right decision. What the future held, she didn't want to think about right now. She had worries enough with Jack.

She stopped at another table and took an order for a glass of wine and a vodka tonic. Seven o'clock and she had three tables full, plus a couple of singles at the bar. It was going to be a busy night. She turned her orders in to her father and he mixed drinks while she poured wine. He pulled two pints of beer and set them on a tray, along with the drinks for the second table. Adding two small bowls of pretzels, Mimi balanced the large platter and expertly hoisted it without a single wobble—another skill she had apparently acquired from her father.

Delivering the wine and vodka first, along with one bowl, she then turned to Evan and Patrick's table. She set the beers down before the two men, then the pretzels.

"I know I've seen you around somewhere. Have we met

before?" Evan asked with a grin. "Maybe I'd recognize your phone number."

Mimi laughed and shook her head at his persistence. He was definitely the sort of guy who liked to test and tease. There was no spark between them, though. *Not like with Ian Berzani,* a voice prompted in her head. She squashed the thought immediately.

"I don't give my phone number out to strange men," she said, wearing a mock frown.

"I'm not strange," Evan said. "Tell her, Patrick."

"It's true. In fact, you're *beyond* strange," Patrick said with a solemn shake of his head.

"Come on! I'm not that bad."

"No, you're worse."

Mimi laughed at that. "I'll be back to check on you in a while."

"My heart will probably stop beating until you return," Evan said soulfully, hand on his chest. His eyes shifted to look over her shoulder and he grinned. "Ian! You're just in time to save me. Tell this gorgeous woman she has to give me her phone number or I'll die."

Mimi heard the name and froze. Her fingers tightened on the tray she held. Slowly, she turned her head and saw Ian Berzani walking toward the table. The speechless immobility she had experienced earlier engulfed her again. Their eyes met and locked as he came closer. He looked just as gorgeous as he had this afternoon. He wore a blue-and-white-checked shirt, and his jeans had been replaced by khaki cargo pants. On his feet, he wore the same battered deck shoes. As he came two steps closer to her, Mimi noticed that his hair was damp and the dark shadow that had been on his jaw earlier was gone. Freshly shaven, the skin there looked smooth and silky. How would it feel under her caress?

Ian reached the table and stood beside her, staring down with an unfathomable expression. His eyes were half lidded, hidden behind thick lashes. Mimi could smell the spicy tang of his aftershave. She breathed it in and felt a strong urge to bury her face in his neck and surround herself in his scent. She clutched the tray to her chest to shield against the attraction she felt.

Ian flicked a glance at Patrick then Evan. "I thought your little black book was filled, McKenzie," he said.

"What book? When I met Mimi, I threw it away," Evan said, his eyes wide.

"Is he bothering you?" Ian asked Mimi, one eyebrow lifted in inquiry. "If he is, I can put his muzzle back on."

"Not especially," Mimi answered. Her voice came out breathless and she winced. She sounded as if she had asthma. She cleared her throat. "What can I get you to drink?"

"An IPA. Thanks."

With a glance at the other two men, Mimi fled the table. As she went, she heard Patrick ask, "Wow, what'd you do to scare her off?"

A few minutes later, Mimi brought Ian's beer to the table. She smiled without meeting his eyes. "Can I get you all anything else?"

"Just stand there and let me adore you," Evan said. He grabbed her hand and kissed it again.

Mimi shook her head in exasperation, tugging to get away from him. "No touching allowed."

"Evan, give it a rest," Ian said.

Mimi's eyes went wide as she looked over at Ian. Had she heard a growl in his voice? Evan and Patrick must have heard something strange, too; they both froze and peered at him. As Ian glowered at his friend, a sly grin grew on Evan's lips. He glanced back and forth between Ian and Mimi, his eyes taking on a speculative gleam. Mimi flushed hot, then cold, and snatched her hand away.

Evan's smile sharpened. "Hmm. Seems I'm too late. Someone else already *has* your number," he said in a silky tone, his eyes back on Ian.

"My phone's been disconnected. Permanently," Mimi said tartly. She had no interest in playing Evan's game, whatever it was. She darted a glance at Ian, whose eyes were locked in battle with Evan's. She couldn't read his expression, but Evan's gleeful mischievousness was easy to see. For a long minute, no one said anything, then Ian abruptly sat back and looked out the window.

"Well, uh, enjoy your drinks," she said feebly.

As she walked away she heard Evan laugh. A flush crept over her cheeks and she couldn't stop herself from glancing back at the three men. Patrick was staring at Ian, who still had his face turned to the window as he sipped his beer. Evan was looking straight at her. Unexpectedly, he winked and she felt her face heat. Mimi snapped back around and walked quickly away. She had a sinking feeling her instincts about Evan had been completely wrong. He was going to cause her all kinds of trouble.

IAN TOOK A LONG DRINK of his beer, then set the glass down. He carefully placed it in the center of the cardboard coaster Mimi had dropped on the table in front of him. He just as carefully avoided meeting Evan's or Patrick's gazes. He had overreacted and he knew it. Seeing Evan touch Mimi had snapped some tether and Ian had reacted without thinking. He also knew that Evan scented blood and would tear after it like the shark that he was. Somehow, Ian would have to endure the ribbing that was sure to come. Finally, he raised his eyes.

"She's hot, isn't she?" Evan asked.

The remark pierced Ian, but he snuffed any visible reaction. "She's all right."

"As the only married man present, I swear that I have no opinion," Patrick said with a laugh.

"You're so whipped," Evan said, slanting a glance at his friend.

"And proud of it." Patrick raised an eyebrow. "Besides, if I said any different, how long would it take you to tell Kate?"

Evan smirked.

"Let's get out of here," Ian said.

"You just got your beer," Patrick said, taking a sip of his own.

"And I think Mimi wants me." Evan's eyes challenged Ian's. "Don't you think so?"

"I'm starved. I missed lunch," Ian said, ignoring the other man. "Let's go down to Gritty's and get a burger."

"They have food here," Evan said. "And the waitress is much better looking. I don't know, though. She is kind of skinny. You think those breasts are real?"

Ian's teeth snapped together, but he refused to be drawn. "They just have bar food here. I want a meal."

A couple sat at the table behind Evan. Mimi walked over to greet them. Her laughter rang clear as she joked with the man and woman. Ian drank again and deliberately avoided looking at her. It didn't matter though. He could picture her face clearly in his head, her curved body and ready smile.

"You don't call a burger 'bar food'?" Evan asked, tilting his head to one side as he looked at Ian.

"I don't see burgers listed here," Patrick said, scanning the menu.

"I'll bet Mimi would whip us up something special if I asked her." Evan smiled and looked over at Mimi as she moved through the bar. His eyes narrowed and his lips pursed. "I bet she knows how to cook."

The beginnings of a headache throbbed at Ian's temples. Evan would go on goading as long as they sat here, probing until he found the soft spot that would send Ian over the edge. Ian had a sinking feeling it wouldn't take him long. Evan was a friend, but tonight, Ian felt like punching him every time he opened his mouth. He had to end the game now.

"Whatever bee you got up your ass about Mimi and me, you're wrong," Ian said, meeting Evan's eyes directly and keeping his own carefully blank. "I've got no interest in starting anything with anyone right now. She could look like Jessica Biel and cook like Rachael Ray and I'd still be out of here in October."

"Seems to me that you've already got something started," Evan said.

"Nope."

"So, I can ask her out?"

"It's no skin off mine," Ian said with a shrug.

Evan squinted at him for a long moment, as if he was not about to back off. Amusement lurked in the back of his green eyes, too. Ian shifted in his seat waiting to duck the next salvo.

Patrick intervened before Evan could speak. "How about we go to the Portside?" he suggested, pushing his beer aside. "I think it's prime-rib night."

"Good enough," Evan said without taking his eyes off Ian. He stood, pulled a money clip out of his pocket and peeled off a twenty. "My treat. I don't get entertained like this very often."

Ian felt the words dig at him, but he absorbed them without comment. He pushed his chair back and stood. Patrick did the same and the three men walked to the door.

Evan detoured to the bar where Mimi stood loading her tray with drinks. "We're going outside to decide the old-fashioned way who gets your number," he announced. "The winner will be back in a while."

She rolled her eyes in response. "It was nice to meet you," she said to Patrick. "Bring your wife next time and leave this guy at home in the kennel."

She didn't look at Ian at all. For some reason, that annoyed him. He squelched the irritation, though. If she wanted to ignore him, that was fine with him. That just made his life simpler. Simple was what he wanted.

Chapter Three

Mimi stood with her arms crossed over her chest, staring out the window overlooking the creek where a trio of ducks flapped and splashed at the edge of the water. The afternoon at the Laughing Gull was quiet, no one out on such a dark and rainy day. Her father stood behind the counter, reading through the sports section. She sighed, turned around and walked over to hitch herself up on a stool in front of the bar.

Her father looked at her from under thick brows. "Why don't you go home? I can handle the crowd in here today."

Mimi propped her elbows on the bar. "What if there's a rush?"

"Ever heard of a telephone?"

With a laugh, she dropped her chin onto her stacked fists. George Green folded his newspaper and set it aside. He poured a glass of cola, added a wedge of lime on the rim and a straw, then set it in front of his daughter.

"This one's on the house."

Mimi lifted her head and pulled the glass toward her, squeezing the lime before dropping it into the dark liquid. She swirled the ice cubes around with the straw, then took a sip. "Thanks."

"So, what's up, Mim?" George asked.

"Nothing," she said with a shrug. "It's the weather."

Her father moved behind the bar to the coffeemaker, bringing the pot over to top off his cup, then set it back on the burner. "I haven't heard a note out of that guitar of yours since you got back."

Mimi darted a glance at him, then looked back at her drink. "I don't play anymore." Silence met her words. She let it stretch to the breaking point, then shot him another look. "Really."

George shook his head and sipped his coffee. "You know," he said meditatively, "I've worked this bar for over thirty years. I've seen drinkers come and go. Some of them drunks, most of them not. I can always pick the drunk out of the crowd, though. Even when they've given up the bottle. There's a need that's always there, always just a second away from tipping them over the edge. I figure that's why they call themselves *recovering* alcoholics. They know that urge will be with them the rest of their lives, whether they give in to it or not."

"I'm not an alcoholic."

"Nope, you're not." George leveled a stare at his daughter. "But if you stop playing music now, you should tell people you're a recovering *musician.*"

"Dad—"

"You've played guitar and sung for twenty years, Mim. You can tell me you've given it up, but the urge will always be with you."

"I *tried,*" Mimi said, sucking down the bitterness that rose in her throat. "For ten years, I did everything I could to make it happen, to be a success. I dragged Jack all over hell and gone and what did I get out of it? *Nothing.*"

"So you didn't become a star, Mim. Big deal. Not many people do and that's the harsh truth. Do they stop playing and singing because the world doesn't listen?"

"But what if playing guitar for me is just like booze for an alcoholic?" She kept her eyes on her glass, poking the straw at the ice cubes in her drink. Finally, she looked up again. "I stopped playing because I can't keep chasing that dream, Dad. I just can't," she said in a whisper.

George put his hands on the bar top and leaned forward, holding her gaze with his. "Then change the dream, Mim. Don't give up your music because other people didn't love it. Give up your music when *you* stop loving it."

A tear welled up and trickled down her cheek and she wiped it away. "Gee, Dad. Don't hold back. Tell me what you really think," she said, trying to make a joke.

George didn't laugh. He leaned back against the coolers and folded his arms across his chest. "You've been moping around here for weeks, grieving over your life like it's dead and gone." His blue eyes speared her intently. "You're a musician. You should play. You should perform. Here."

"What?" Mimi stared at him, eyes wide at the idea.

"I'll even pay you a percentage of the take that night." He grinned at her. "I'll make you a better deal than you'll get in any other bar in town."

As George was making his offer, the door burst open and Jack dashed inside, shaking rain off his hair like a dog. "Hi, Mom. Hi, Grandpop." He dumped his backpack on the floor and dropped his raincoat on top of it. Climbing on to a stool next to Mimi, he asked, "What's a better deal?"

"I told your mom I'd pay her if she sang in the bar."

"Are you gonna sing?" Jack asked, his eyes lighting up.

"No! I—"

"She needs some persuading," George said with a wink to his grandson. "She's afraid she'll stink."

"No, you won't, Mom. That'd be great! When are you gonna do it? You should do that mermaid song. And—"

"Slow down," Mimi said with a laugh. His excitement was infectious. "I'll think about it. Okay?"

The idea was unsettling. She had spent a lot of time over the past few months convincing herself that her life as a musician was over. Giving up music had been the hardest thing she had ever done in her twenty-seven years. Now her father was insisting that she didn't have to cut it out of her life completely. That she *shouldn't*. The idea was so tempting, it hurt. Was her father right? Slowly, an excitement that had been missing for months began to rise inside. She squelched it, but it was not so easily suppressed.

"You should do it, Mom." Jack's eyes were filled with a solemn certainty she had a hard time resisting.

"You should, Mim," George added as he filled up a glass with soda and added a straw. He handed it to his grandson. "You're not supposed to sit at the bar, kid."

"Then why'd you give me a glass?" Jack asked. He sucked on the straw and looked around him. "Besides, who's gonna know?"

"*I* know, smart guy," George said, then squirted more soda in the glass. "What if the cops came in? I'd be busted for serving minors."

"I doubt it," Jack said with a scoff.

Mimi reached out to brush his hair off his forehead, but Jack ducked away from her hand. He was getting to the stage where he didn't want to be touched anymore and her heart broke every time he evaded her caresses. The only time he let her cuddle him was when they read together at night. She supposed that would soon end, as well. The price of growing up that she paid, not Jack.

"How was school?" Mimi asked.

"The usual." Her son shrugged. "It sucked."

The door opened again and four people walked in, heading directly toward the tables near the windows. They were laughing and talking, their bright red and yellow raincoats making a cheerful scene against the dreary weather.

Jack took advantage of the distraction, hopping off the stool and picking up his backpack and coat. "I'm gonna go play on the computer."

"Homework first."

"Aw, Mom. I can do it later." Then he was out the door.

Mimi frowned after him.

"Go help Jack with his homework," George said. "I'll call if it gets busy."

"Thanks, Dad."

Mimi spun off her stool and followed her son. Every day the answer to her question about school was the same. Every afternoon they struggled through homework. *We just have to get through the next week,* she thought as she slipped into her raincoat at the door. Then they would have a few months of respite before the ordeal started all over again. Maybe she should look into getting him a tutor. The thought made her grimace. She knew exactly how Jack would take that suggestion. Still, he just wasn't thriving the way she thought he should. The way she *hoped* he would, anyway.

Mimi pushed the bar door open and stepped out into the rain, swallowing down the burgeoning guilt she felt. Despite what her parents said, she knew that Jack's troubles were her fault. What did she expect from a nine-year-old vagabond?

Mimi shook her head as she splashed through the puddles to her parents' house. The rain seemed to fall from all directions. Wind blew the water around in circles before each raindrop splashed into the puddles on the sidewalk. She dashed up the steps to the back door, pushing her hood off under the shelter of the porch. There, one hand on the doorknob, she paused. Through the lace curtain she could see Jack and her mother seated at the kitchen table.

Jack was stuffing a chocolate-chip cookie in his mouth. Claire set a glass of milk in front of him, next to a plate holding three more cookies. Mimi saw her run a hand over her grandson's hair, gently pushing the fringe out of his eyes. That Jack didn't pull away or flinch amazed and gratified Mimi. Claire must have said something to Jack, because he laughed, showing a mouth full of cookie before covering it with one hand. Mimi saw her mother frown, then laugh, too. They looked so alike just then, both alive with laughter and happiness.

Mimi sighed and closed her eyes for a moment. Tears pricked at the back of her lids. Jack was happy at least *some* of the time. Maybe her parents were right; he just needed a little more time to settle into their life and catch up with his classmates. She would talk to his teachers again, she decided. They might have suggestions for what could be done to help Jack do better and enjoy school.

In the meantime, she would try harder to help Jack find his way in this new, strange world. Summer was nearly here. Together they would make Crab Creek home. One place she could start was to give them both back the music that had surrounded their lives. He loved it as much as she did. Maybe if she played, it would give a piece of their old life back to him.

Her lips twisted in a grimace. She was making justifications, but it was still a good idea. They were *both* unhappy, she had to admit. It was time she did something to change that. She turned the doorknob and stepped inside the house.

"Hey, there. Did you leave any cookies for me?"

"IAN! DON'T FORGET TO take these," Elaine Berzani called to her eldest son before he pulled the office door shut behind him. A small woman with bright red hair and clear gray eyes, she didn't look old enough to have four grown children. Especially when one of them was Ian's age.

Ian turned back and saw her waving a sheaf of papers at him. "Give those to Patrick. He's in charge of Sid's project now. Not me."

Elaine frowned at the papers. "Are you sure? He said you knew more about it than he did."

"Well, it's time for him to learn more than me."

With pursed lips, Elaine shook her head. "All right, but I'm sending him to you first if he has problems."

"Yes, Mother. Thank you, Mother. Goodbye, Mother," Ian said as he closed the door. Through the glass, he caught a glimpse of her smile.

Ian slipped on his sunglasses and headed across the boatyard to the docks. The day had dawned clear and bright, a welcome change from the rain of the past three days. A light breeze swirled around Ian as he walked away from the office. The pungent odor of seaweed and barnacles wafted through the air as he passed the travel-lift, which had a boat suspended in its slings. Bart, the lift operator, was using a pressure washer to hose off a coating of slime and grass from the bottom of a large cabin cruiser. Piles of barnacles lay under the shaft where he had scraped the metal clean of the clinging creatures.

Saturday mornings the yard did short-hauls—a quick bottom-clean and inspection for boats that didn't need a new coat of paint or any other major work. Once they were done, the yard would quiet for the rest of the weekend.

"Is that the last one?" Ian called out to Bart over the low buzz of the pump.

The older man stopped the jet of water. "Nope. We've got one more, but we're going to let 'er hang for the weekend. They're drillin' a hole for a new transducer. Should take about an hour to finish up. I'll drop 'er in first thing Monday morning.''

"Good enough." Ian nodded. Bart started the pressure washer again, sending a spray of water ricocheting from the hull in a rainbow mist of color.

Ian continued on his path to the docks. Patrick's sailing school was starting in an hour, but Ian hoped to get a few things done before the kids arrived. As he got near the water's edge, he noticed a familiar figure crouched there. Jack Green was dressed differently today, but the baggy fit of the clothes was the same. Ian changed course and walked up behind him.

"Hey, kid. What's up?"

Jack stiffened and rose. "I wasn't doing noth—"

"*Any*thing. Yeah, where have I heard that before?" Ian pushed his sunglasses up on his head and surveyed the child. "I thought we agreed you weren't going to play around here anymore."

"I'm not *playing*," the boy said, spitting the word out as if it was coated in vinegar. "I'm nine."

"Hmm." Ian held back a smile. "Then what're you doing? If you don't mind my asking."

The kid shrugged and looked down.

"What's the matter, don't you have anything better to do than splash around in the mud?"

"I've got plenty to do."

"Really?" Ian crossed his arms over his chest. He had seen a brief flash of emotion flicker across the boy's face. Was it fear? Anger? Ian rejected those, deciding it was something closer to pain, maybe loneliness. He felt a twinge of sympathy. It had to be hard coming to a new place and starting over with no friends. Especially with a chip on your shoulder the size of Mississippi.

"You'd better come with me."

"You don't have to tell my mom," Jack said sullenly. "I won't come back."

Ian shook his head. "Look, if you're going to hang around the yard, you're going to have to work, like everybody else."

"Work? I'm a kid."

"So, you'll do kid's work," Ian said calmly. He turned and walked a few steps away before turning back. "Come on," he said. "I haven't got all day."

Jack stared at him, eyes wary behind his fringe of shaggy hair. Ian stood silent and patient, letting the boy make his own decision. Slowly, the wariness was replaced with curiosity. Ian hid another smile as Jack frowned.

"I'm not gonna be nobody's slave."

"Trust me," Ian said with a chuckle. "Nobody would buy a runt like you."

"I'm not a runt." Jack's frown was halfhearted.

Ian took two steps toward the boy, so that he loomed over him. He put one hand on the sandy-brown head, the other on his own, then examined the distance between his hands.

"I'd say you're about average size for a runt."

"I'm tall for my age." The boy's blue eyes were clear, and for the first time since they had met, held a spark of friendly humor.

"And skinny, too, but that's no selling point."

Jack grinned, and Ian felt as if he had won something precious. He flipped his sunglasses down to cover any triumph that might show in his eyes. "Come on, runt. There's work to be done."

He led Jack over to the piers where Patrick was setting up the boats for the sailing school. With his usual ease, Evan had charmed someone into donating the money to buy a half-dozen Optimist sailing dinghies. Somewhere else, Patrick had cadged five more, so they had a fleet of eleven. They were pulled up on the dock in a row behind jumbled piles of sails, masts, daggerboards and rudders. Evan had told Patrick he could get money for four more new boats midway through the summer. Who would have the pleasure of donating those funds, Ian didn't ask. He was merely impressed by Evan's ability to charm money out of trees.

"Hey, I shanghaied a worker," Ian called out to Patrick.

His brother looked up from where he stood on the dock, setting a mast in place on one of the dinghies. "Looks a little skinny to me," Patrick said as they came closer.

"Best I could find on short notice." Ian nudged Jack and grinned. Jack elbowed him back, shooting him a sideways glare. "But he's got a few muscles on him." Ian put a hand on Jack's shoulder and introduced the two. "Patty, this is Jack Green. Jack, this is my little brother, Patrick."

Patrick offered his hand and the two solemnly shook. "Pleased to meet you, Jack. You here to sail today?"

Jack shook his head. "I'm supposed to work."

"Jack's nine. He doesn't *play*," Ian said, giving Jack's shoulder a teasing shake. "He's been hanging around the yard, so I figured he needed a job."

"Do you know anything about sailboats, Jack?"

"Some." He shrugged. "They don't have motors. And they're slow."

Patrick hooted with laughter. "That's where you're wrong, kiddo. Some sailboats are as fast as powerboats and a whole lot more fun."

"Patrick races sailboats," Ian said.

"Where?"

"On the ocean and here on the Bay."

Jack squinted up at Patrick. "Really fast?"

"Really, *really* fast. Remind me later and I'll show you some videos."

"In the meantime, what needs to be done here?" Ian asked.

"The rest of these masts need to be stepped, then we can hang the booms and run the rigging. I want everything set up before the kids get here. Next time, we'll teach them how to do it themselves."

Ian and Jack formed a team, putting masts upright on the small boats, hanging the booms and reeving the main sheets through the blocks. Jack was a fast learner, following Ian's directions, watching what Ian did and copying it exactly. He even started to anticipate what came next, which impressed Ian. Maybe the kid wasn't so bad after all. Most of his orneriness was probably due to boredom. Ian decided a good challenge would keep him from being such a pain.

"Okay, first thing to learn on a boat is that everything has a proper name. The pointy end is the bow and the flat end is the stern. Got it?"

Jack stood straight and looked over the little boat. "They're both kinda flat."

"The *wider* flat end is the stern," Ian said, rubbing a hand over Jack's head. "Smart-ass."

Jack giggled, then nodded. "Bow and stern."

"Second thing to learn is port and starboard. This is port," Ian said, pointing to the right side of the boat as they faced the bow. "The other side's starboard."

"Why?"

"You want the long answer or the short one?"

Jack stuck his lower lip out in thought. "The short one, I guess."

"Starboard is the old way of saying 'steering-board,' because this side of the ship was where the rudder was mounted, before they started putting the rudder in the middle of the boat. Port used to be called larboard, for lee-board, meaning the board that kept the boat running straight. It was also the side they tied to the dock because it didn't have the rudder in the way. Larboard and starboard sounded too much alike, so the name got changed to port."

Jack frowned. "That's a long short answer and it's *still* confusing."

"Not really." He walked over to the boy and turned him around so he was facing the stern of the boat. "Which direction is port now?"

Jack looked up at him, a frown on his face. He hesitated, then cautiously pointed to the left side of the boat. Ian squeezed his shoulder briefly and released him.

"Exactly. It's always the same."

"Always?" Jack sounded doubtful. "No matter what?"

"No matter what. No matter what direction you're facing. Same as the bow and stern are always the same."

Jack and Ian continued rigging the boats and Ian kept adding terminology for the parts of the boat as they worked. Noticing that Jack mumbled the words under his breath as he worked, Ian hid a smile. But the kid used the new terms correctly, rarely getting one wrong.

"Has A&E gotten so desperate that it's using child labor?"

Ian and Jack looked up to see Evan McKenzie standing with his hands on his hips, grinning at them. He was dressed much as they were in baggy shorts, T-shirt and flip-flops. His faded green shirt bore the logo of a local surf shop.

"Since you didn't bother to show up on time, McKenzie, we had to do something." Ian straightened and held out a hand in greeting. "He works harder than you do, too."

One blond eyebrow arched above the rim of his sunglasses. "I never work hard, Berzani. I'm here to supervise."

"Jack, this is Evan. He's one of the instructors for this adventure," Ian said. "Evan, this is Jack Green from down the street."

Evan tipped his sunglasses down his nose to scrutinize the boy as he held out his hand. They shook. "Your mom's Mimi Green?" The boy nodded and Evan smiled. "She's cool."

Jack shrugged, but Ian could tell the compliment pleased him.

Evan looked over at Ian, his eyes glinting with devilish humor. "I thought you weren't interested in starting anything?"

Ian scowled, but kept silent. There was nothing he could say now, not with Jack right here listening. Evan smirked and slid his sunglasses back into place as he surveyed the boats lined up on the dock.

"Good. Looks like you guys are just about done."

At that moment, Patrick joined them. "About time you turned up, McKenzie. What took you so long?"

"Things went a little long last night," Evan said with a sly grin.

"As in early this morning." Patrick's tone was dry.

"What can I say? Kippy wouldn't let me leave."

"I don't know what you see in that woman," Patrick said, shaking his head. "All she talks about is her hair, her clothes or the latest gunk she puts on her face."

Evan pursed his lips. "I'm not in it for the conversation. It's all about the—"

Ian cleared his throat, jerking his head toward Jack. All three men looked down to see the boy grinning up at them. That he had caught the gist of their conversation was obvious.

"Kids these days," Evan muttered, just as three boys and a girl ran down the ramp onto the dock.

Patrick headed off to meet them, warning that they shouldn't run on the piers. Ian checked his watch and saw that it was time for class to begin.

"Give me a hand with these life jackets," Ian said to the boy.

Jack followed and Ian gave him five of the small jackets to carry, taking the other six himself. He led the way up to the group of chattering kids flocking around Patrick. Evan stood back, arms folded over his chest, casting a dubious glance over the mayhem.

As Patrick greeted the kids and their parents, Ian stood to one side with Jack. He slid a glance at the boy and found him watching the other children with a solemn expression that gave nothing away. After Patrick shooed the parents off the docks, he gave the children a brief lecture about what today's class would cover. Ian had to laugh at this: the kids paid no attention to the words. They were too entranced by the little boats strung out neatly along the dock.

Patrick motioned to Ian and he began distributing the flotation devices, one to each student. Jack followed Ian, silently handing over the jackets he held until there was one left. As Patrick demonstrated how to put the vests on safely, Jack pushed that last PFD at Ian.

"What? That's too small. It's not going to fit me," Ian said.

"Who should I give it to?"

"Looks runt-size. Try it on."

"Me?"

"Nobody gets in a boat without a life jacket. Doesn't matter if you know how to swim or not." When Jack opened his mouth to protest, Ian added, "Hey, I don't make the rules, I just enforce them."

"But I'm not getting in a boat," Jack said, looking up at Ian. His face was scrunched into a frown.

"Why not?"

"I didn't sign up for class," Jack said quietly.

His eyes refused to meet Ian's. Ian laid a gentle hand on his shoulder, turning him to face the class that was assembled on the dock. Patrick had the other kids lined up, each at the bow of one of the small dinghies. There was one boat without a child next to it. Its red-and-yellow-striped sail fluttered in the breeze.

"Look. There's one boat left. Somebody must have known you were coming."

Jack stood still, staring at the other children, then turned his face up to Ian. "Really?" he asked, his voice nearly a whisper. Astonished hope filled his blue eyes and it was all Ian could do not to hug the boy. He took the life jacket out of Jack's tight grip and held it open for him.

"Come on, runt," he said gruffly. "You're holding up the show."

In seconds the buckles were clipped, straps adjusted and Jack stood in place with the other ten students ready for class. Ian felt a lump rise in his throat as he watched how attentively Jack listened to Patrick's instructions. When Jack looked over his shoulder and grinned—pure delight lighting his face like Fourth of July in the evening sky—Ian laughed. He was starting to like this kid. He really was.

Chapter Four

Mimi worked her way frantically down the street. Stopping at an alley, she peered down the length of it. All she saw were trash cans and overgrown bushes. "Jack!" she yelled.

Nothing moved. Crossing the road, she stood at the cyclone fence that surrounded A&E Marine, scanning between the rows of boats neatly propped up on blue metal stands. It was relatively quiet this Saturday morning. A man in a baggy white work suit was sanding the hull of a sailboat. A dog chased a tennis ball thrown from somewhere. She caught sight of the water's edge here and there between the row of large, uniformly gray buildings, but no sign of a nine-year-old child. Crossing the street again, she walked farther down, craning her neck to look into backyards, behind hedges, anyplace a boy might explore or hide.

After breakfast that morning, Jack was supposed to have gone to his room to study—or at least pretend to study. At ten o'clock, Mimi had decided to check on his progress. She found his math book and science lessons in his unopened backpack hidden under a pile of yesterday's clothes: he hadn't even made a start on his homework. She called for him. No answer. Neither her mother nor father had seen him in the house or out in the yard. He had at least two overdue book reports to write for English and a second shot at a take-home math exam to help bring his grade up. Somehow he had escaped and run off. Irritated with his irresponsibility and cunning, Mimi had gone looking for him.

After an hour of fruitless searching, her aggravation had evolved to worry, then panic. She had been all around the neighborhood: the park, the nearby grocery store, the strip mall where she had seen other kids hanging out. No trace of him anywhere. She crossed the road yet again and came to the boatyard's main entrance. The marina lay near the bottom of her list of likely places. Jack had promised her that he would not go there again. Then again, he had made this vow under duress. He might sneak in there just because it was forbidden and a good hideout.

The gate was wide open, beckoning, yet Mimi hesitated. She must have been by the place hundreds of times, but could not remember actually going inside it, not even in high school when she and Anna had hung out together. This was Ian Berzani's domain, and going inside felt like sneaking into enemy territory. What if she saw him? Or he saw her?

Stop being a wuss, she told herself. *What if Jack's in there?*

Boldly, she stepped across the gravel parking lot, each footfall making a loud crunch. She made her way toward the water, past the sheds. Each building had a sign on it: Canvas Shop, Wood Shop, Machine Shop. For a place that bustled with chaos during the workweek, it seemed rather tidy. About a dozen cars were parked near the last and smallest building. Office, the sign read. Like the others, it was closed and deserted.

Beyond the office, a large, blue boat-lift stood idle on a concrete pad. A small powerboat hung in the canvas slings, a ladder propped against one side. No one was there either, but beyond it Mimi could hear someone shouting over the roar of an outboard motor. Something was going on out there. Mimi followed the path and ramp that led down to the docks. She saw nine-year-old-size tracks in the mud on the shoreline.

The shouts became louder, carrying over the water and rows of boats tied to the dock. There were children's voices, too. At the intersection of two docks, she turned left and saw about a dozen brightly colored sails—fuchsia, yellow, turquoise, orange—zipping around a patch of sheltered water. The sun reflected from the water into her eyes, but she recognized the sturdy little gaff-rigged sailboats and the emblems on the sails: Optimist dinghies. She had sailed them at summer camp when she was about twelve.

Mimi quickened her steps down the dock, sure that the boats had lured her son and fearing that his curiosity and audacity might get him into trouble. At the end of the dock, she spied a tall figure standing facing away from her, back-lit by the sunshine and dazzling colors. Ian Berzani. She stopped in her tracks. A kind of raw heat seemed to radiate from him, flashing across her skin. Her mouth went dry.

Despite the baggy tan shorts and gray T-shirt he wore, Mimi was all too conscious of his lean strength. His arms were crossed over his chest, pulling the soft cotton shirt taut across the muscles along his back and shoulders. His bare legs, at least the length below the hemline of his shorts, were equally well muscled. He wore black flip-flops, his feet planted wide on the wood decking. The urge to go up to him and run her hands over his strong back was intense.

Abruptly, Ian turned his head and looked over his shoulder, straight at her. Dark sunglasses hid his eyes, but his lips tightened into a thin line as his arms dropped to his sides. He looked gorgeous. And obviously unhappy to see her. She had seen the same scowl of pain, irritation or *some*thing the two times they had met before. Mimi bit her lip and forced herself to walk toward him.

"Morning," he said with a nod, as he stuck his hands into the pockets of his shorts.

"Good morning. I'm looking for Jack." Her voice was cool, her words clipped.

Ian said nothing. He looked back at the fleet of boats bobbing up and down in the water. There wasn't much wind, but the kids used what there was to create maximum chaos, tacking and jibing with abandon. Several near collisions brought screams of laughter floating across the water. Two small motorboats circled the dinghies. Mimi saw Patrick in one and Evan McKenzie in the other. They were calling out instructions to the youngsters, most of which went unheeded.

She waited for Ian to say something, to make any sign showing that he remembered she was there. "Have you seen him?" she asked, impatient with his silence, with his ignoring her.

One hand came out of his pocket and he pointed to the Optimists. "Third boat from the right. The one with the red-and-yellow-striped sail."

She shielded her eyes against the sun and instantly recognized Jack. One hand on the tiller and one on the mainsheet, his back was to her. His shoulders were set, head cocked forward in that way he had when he was intent on something.

"What is he *doing* out there?" she asked, her voice rising to a squeak.

"Learning to sail."

"I can see *that*. Who let him?"

"He was hanging around here again. And if he doesn't pull the bow around he's going to… Ouch, accidental jibe.

Managed not to knock himself in the head, though. Nice work, runt!" he called out, his hands cupped around his mouth.

Jack untangled himself from the mainsheet, set the boat on a collision course with a piling and looked over at Ian. A wide grin split his face as he flapped his hand in a gesture that dismissed Ian and the interference of the shoreside world. He spied his mother, then turned around and waved wildly, recklessly rocking the little boat.

Mimi waved back, willing him with a grimace to be more careful. She crossed her arms over her chest and turned to face Ian. "*You* put him in that boat?" she demanded.

He didn't even glance her way. "We had an extra one, so I thought he'd enjoy a sailing lesson."

"You should have called me first."

"I didn't think you'd mind. He's wearing a life jacket and Patrick's—"

"He's supposed to be at home doing his schoolwork."

"On Saturday morning?"

His question, which implied that she was impossibly strict, maddened her. "I've spent the past two hours looking all over for him."

"Was I supposed to know that?" he asked with a shrug that only made her angrier.

"No, because you didn't call me and ask my permission," Mimi said, glaring at him.

"I asked him if he had anything to do. He didn't mention homework."

"Of course not! He's nine!"

Ian pushed his sunglasses to the top of his head, put his hands on his hips and faced her. "What do you—"

"Mom! Did you see me?" Jack's piercing cry startled them both. He had somehow managed to avoid the piling. Now he was about to ram the dock a few feet away.

Sucking in a breath, Mimi put her hands out and stepped forward. Ian was quicker. He reached out and caught the dinghy mast with one hand. The small boat gracefully bumped the dock and stopped.

"That was about the sloppiest jibe I've ever seen, runt," Ian said. "You almost beaned yourself with the boom."

Runt? Mimi frowned. Where had that nickname come from? She almost objected, except that Jack didn't seem to mind. His brown hair was pushed back away from his eyes. Happiness danced in their blue depths.

"I didn't mean to do it," Jack said. "I pulled the tiller instead of pushing it."

"Try doing it on purpose next time." Ian's advice was accompanied by a wry smile that seemed to mirror Jack's. "You still have another twenty minutes of sailing time. Unless you're tired of it."

"No way! Give me a push off. Mom, watch this!"

Mimi was about to remind him about his homework, but thought better of it. Jack seemed to have forgotten all his cares and obligations. Ian grabbed the boom and turned the boat, then gave the stern of the dinghy a gentle shove with his foot. Jack wiggled the tiller and pulled in the mainsheet. The light breeze filled the sail, scooting his boat across the water toward the center of the fleet.

"Has he sailed before?" Ian asked, his eyes on the boy.

"No. Not that I know of."

"He catches on quick. Kid's a natural."

The fact that Ian seemed almost proud of this discovery, as if he had something to do with it, irked Mimi even more. "Great! Why don't you teach him long division or how to write a book report on *Treasure Island?*"

He turned back to face her, and Ian's dark gaze met hers

for a long moment. Finally, he sighed. "He needs to be in this class, Mimi."

"You're telling me how to raise my son? Well, then, tell me, Dr. Spock, what's more important—passing fourth grade or learning to sail?"

"It's not that simple."

"Of course it's not. Parenting is never simple. There are rules I have to enforce. And I have to be his best friend, too. Try *that* balancing act sometime."

Ian shook his head. He looked away for a second, out over the water, then back at her. When he spoke, his tone was even and calm. "Jack is rude, has no respect for anyone—especially adults—and ignores what he doesn't want to hear. If he doesn't change his attitude, he's going to end up in real trouble."

Mimi sucked in a breath to speak, but Ian didn't stop there.

"His problem is that he's smart, Mimi, and he's bored out of his skull. Maybe I see that because I was the same way at his age. He needs to be challenged, and since school's not doing it for him, maybe sailing will."

"You've spent an hour with my son and suddenly you're the expert," Mimi said furiously. "What gives you—"

Before she could finish, the first of the dinghies arrived at the dock. The wind had picked up during their argument. The girl in the boat squealed as she came in too fast, let go of the tiller and put her hands over her eyes. The dinghy immediately rounded up into the wind, slowed down and slewed sideways against the dock. Ian turned and caught the mast, bringing the boat to a gentle halt. The girl uncovered her eyes.

"I did it!"

"Excellent job," Ian said as he crouched down to her level. "Next time we'll try it with your eyes open."

Mimi watched as the girl giggled and crawled out of the boat. She didn't want to be impressed with Ian: how he could tease, encourage and correct a child without squelching her spirit. He might know something about children and sailing. That didn't qualify him to solve Jack's problems.

Ian handed the girl the bowline and pointed her up the pier. "Don't drop this. Just pull the boat up farther and we'll drag it up on deck in a minute."

She obeyed orders just as a second and third boat arrived at the dock. Their landings were little better than the first. Given the wind direction and speed, the kids that panicked and dropped the tiller fared better than those who clung on, trying to control their landings. Left alone, the sturdy Optimists performed their trick of stalling and sliding into the dock.

Rather than stew in her irritation, Mimi decided to pitch in. She reached out and grabbed one boat before it could crash against its neighbor. The kid in it had a look of terror on his face.

She smiled reassuringly. "You forgot to use your emergency brake."

Once the danger passed, the boy relaxed. "I need more practice," he said breathlessly. He hopped out of the boat and Mimi directed him to join the other children waiting to haul their crafts out of the water.

Jack came in next. His jaw was set in concentration as he worked the tiller. His boat also came in at ramming speed, but Ian caught it easily. "You have to let the main out when you come in," he said. "Spill wind so that you slow down, then you can push the rudder over and come alongside."

"That was so cool!" Jack nearly bounced out of the dinghy and up onto the dock. "Mom, did you see? I was flying out there! Sailboats are fast. Did you know—"

"Hold up there, runt. Let's get everybody stowed and then you can tell her all about it."

Patrick and Evan herded the last two wayward boats in, then tied up their powerboats at one end of the dock. Everyone joined in hoisting the dinghies out of the water. It was mass confusion with excited children darting around, jostling each other, shouting commentary. Parents began to show up, as well, and chaos briefly reigned again.

Patrick got things under control quickly with a short, sharp blast from the whistle he had around his neck. "All right! You're free to go today, but next week you're all going to step the masts and rig the boat yourselves and down-rig them at the end of the day."

Scattered chatter ensued as the group of adults and children began to disperse. Patrick moved through the crowd of kids and parents, talking to each individually. Evan worked the crowd, too, obviously acquainted with most of the adults there. Mimi stood on the sidelines, waiting for Jack. He was describing some feat he had performed to Ian with wide, sweeping hand gestures. She saw Ian smile, then laugh, his head tipped down to the boy.

Jack had not been this excited in weeks, or even months. Maybe Ian was right about one thing: her son *was* bored. Mimi chewed her lower lip as she watched them together. Maybe. But sailing was no substitute for homework. Once school was over, she would consider letting him come back. Mimi sighed. She wished he had found interest in something that didn't involve Ian Berzani. It was time to get them both out of here.

As Jack told his tale about his narrow escape from a crash with two other boats, Ian glanced at Jack's mother. Mimi was still mad, that much was clear. The set of her shoulders, arms folded tightly across her chest, said it all.

But what Jack needed was just as obvious. A good education meant more than books and homework, especially in Jack's case. Couldn't she see that? Ian didn't regret telling her what he thought; if it annoyed her, too bad. Putting the kid on the right track was worth any amount of anger.

Mimi joined them, her eyes on her son. "Hey, are you ready to leave, kiddo?"

"I've gotta help take the masts—"

"You don't have to, runt. If your mother wants you to go with her, that's okay."

"But—"

"You've been hanging around here long enough," Mimi said, ruffling her son's hair. "And it's past time for lunch."

At that moment, Evan McKenzie came over and draped an arm over Mimi's shoulder. "Hey, gorgeous. I knew you'd find me again somewhere."

Mimi looked pointedly at Evan's arm, then lifted it off her shoulder as though it were a dirty wet rag. "Actually, I was hoping to leave before you saw me."

Evan pulled away with a laugh. "Ouch. Rejected again."

Ian's teeth clamped tightly together and a muscle twitched in his jaw. His heated response was instinctive, but this time, he kept his mouth shut. Evan grinned at him, teeth glinting like a friendly, man-eating shark's. He slipped his sunglasses down off his nose and winked, then slid them back into place.

"You all right, Berzani? You're looking a little green. Maybe you should lie down for a bit."

Patrick joined them at that moment and spared Ian the trouble of thinking up a civil reply. "Hey, Mimi. Jack did great out there."

"I can stay and help take the masts down," Jack insisted. "I can do—"

"Hold on there, sailor." Patrick put his hand out to stop the words spilling out of the boy. "Lunch first, then back to work."

"We'd better let these guys eat, Jack," Mimi said. "I'm sure Grandmom has lunch waiting for us, too."

"No, stay! Join us for lunch," Evan said. "Then Ian and Jack can put the dinghies to bed while you and I discuss our future."

Ian pretended not to hear this. He was damned if he'd let McKenzie make him look like a fool again. To his chagrin, Patrick seconded the invitation.

"Anna said she might come down. She'd love to see you," Patrick said. "You can meet my wife, too."

"Oh, I—"

"Kate's coming?" Evan asked, eyebrows snapping down in a frown. His voice was a growl of displeasure as he glared at Patrick. "You said she wasn't. You *promised*."

"I lied," Patrick said with a grin. "Look, here they are now."

At the head of the dock, Ian saw Patrick's wife, Kate, carrying their eight-month-old daughter in her arms. Anna strolled down the dock at her side. In sundresses and sandals, the two women looked as festive as the sails on the dinghies. Kate's yellow gingham dress matched the one her daughter wore. Anna, in turquoise, her bright red hair flaming in the sun, was even more striking.

A screech of glee from the baby echoed across the dock as Evan ducked behind Ian and Patrick. "Damn," he muttered. "I've been spotted."

"I think you're wrong, Patty," Ian said with a grin, part of his good humor restored by seeing Evan squirm. "I think Beth's eyesight is pretty good. She had him at fifty yards."

As the women came closer, Anna was next to let out a shrill cry of happiness. "Oh, my God, Mimi! Is it really you?"

The two women launched themselves toward each other in a frenzy of hugs, kisses, laughter and tears. A wave of envy swept through Ian. He doubted he would ever get that kind of reception from Mimi.

While Anna and Mimi played catch-up, Patrick stepped forward to kiss Kate and his baby. Beth was squirming and fussing unhappily. She craned her neck around her father, ignoring his affection, and squealed again when she saw Evan. Her arms reached out for him.

"All right, all right," Evan said with a sigh. He held out his arms, reluctance in every line of his body. "Let's get this over with, Betsy Wetsy."

The baby cooed as Kate passed her over. Once in his embrace, Beth nestled into Evan's neck, small hands grasping his T-shirt, drool dampening his shoulder.

"Don't be jealous," Evan said to Mimi and Anna with a grin. "All the girls have the same problem around me."

As Beth gurgled up at Evan, Anna shook her head in dismay. "That is the *weirdest* thing I've ever seen. If she's attracted to Evan now, what kind of guy is she going to bring home when she's sixteen?"

Everyone laughed except Evan. "Obviously, someone with charm, wit and good taste," he said, his tone cool.

"Now I *am* terrified," Kate said dryly.

Ian chuckled as Evan frowned. "It's good to have you around, Annie," he said and slung an arm across his sister's shoulders. "Somebody's got to corral McKenzie."

"Only too happy to help." She kissed Ian on the cheek and looked at the rest of the group. "Come on. Kate and I set lunch out on the picnic tables by the office," she said. "Oh! Kate, did you meet Mimi?"

Ian watched as Mimi smiled brightly at Kate and shook her hand. He swallowed down irritation as she began chatting easily with the other woman and they moved up the dock. Yet another person she was happy to be with—anyone other than him. Jack sauntered along at his mother's heels. Evan followed, carrying Beth like a fragile vase that might shatter at any moment, with Patrick at his side. Ian and Anna brought up the rear.

Ian watched Beth gurgling and clutching at Evan's shoulder, reaching up for his nose and glasses. "You know, with that baby, Evan could almost pass for a father."

"Are you kidding?" Anna asked, shooting him a laughter-filled glance. "He barely passes for a human being."

Jack dropped back and bounced up beside Ian. "That was awesome out there," he said. "Did you see it when that kid almost ran into me? I turned just in time."

Ian smiled as he listened to Jack recount his exploits in the Optimist. What a different kid he was now than only a few hours ago. He was floating about a foot off the ground, high on his morning's adventure in a sailboat. As if he might be in danger of drifting away on his own delight, Jack grabbed Ian's hand. Ian clasped the smaller one carefully, letting the boy frisk along at his side and listening to his stream of chatter.

As they continued, Jack kept glancing at Anna, frowning slightly, his lower lip pushed out. "Is that your girlfriend?" he finally asked.

"This?" Ian looked over at Anna. "Naw, this is my little sister, Anna. Annie, this is Jack Green, Mimi's kid."

"Really?" Anna said, obviously surprised. "How old are you?"

"I'm nine."

She looked intently at the boy, like he was an endangered species on display at the zoo. Instead of flinching, Jack locked his gaze with hers.

Ian tightened his arm around Anna's shoulder. "It's rude to stare," he said in a mock whisper.

"He started it," Anna said.

"I don't think so," Ian said. "*You* did."

"Shut up. If I quit now, he wins."

A grin started to steal across Jack's face, but he kept his eyes fixed on Anna's. Suddenly, she crossed her eyes and stuck out her tongue. Jack began to giggle, then he blinked. "No fair! You made me laugh."

Anna let out a crow of triumph. "The winner and still champion of the stare-down!"

Jack laughed again, while trying to compose a frown on his face. He tugged on Ian's hand. "She cheated."

"Yeah," Ian agreed. "Girls do that."

They went up the ramp to shore and the group shuffled itself into a new configuration. Evan passed Beth back to her mother. Anna asked Patrick how many more kids they planned to have. Jack took his mother's hand and Ian found himself linked to Mimi with the boy between them. Mimi shot him a quick look but didn't say a word.

Of course, Evan had to notice and make a remark. "Hmm. Looks like a family unit to me," he said, a smirk on his face.

"McKenzie, can't you find something else to meddle in?" Ian asked irritably.

Mimi looked at them both, but was silent. As the group surrounded the picnic tables—one piled with food and drink, the other cleared for dining—Ian dropped Jack's hand and drifted a few steps away. Jack, Mimi and Anna dished up lunch for themselves. Kate sat with the baby. After Mimi and Jack left the food table, Ian took a plate and slowly filled it. Out of the corner of his eye, he watched the seating arrangement take form.

The table had benches fixed on either side, enough for six adults. It would be a slight squeeze with the addition of Jack. Beth would sit on her mother's knee. Mimi sat on the other side of the table from Kate, with Jack on the end. Then Anna sat opposite Mimi. Patrick brought a plate a food for his wife and the baby. As if to make Ian's life difficult, his brother sat next to Anna. That left one vacancy for Evan or Ian right next to Mimi.

"I'll flip you for it," Evan offered, holding out a quarter. "Tails, I sit next to her. Heads, you get to."

"Don't be such a jerk, McKenzie," Ian said with a growl.

He put his plate beside Mimi's, despite the fact that he wished he could sit anywhere else. Ian knew he couldn't handle it if Evan spent their entire lunch flirting with her. He would end up killing the smart-ass. Mimi kept her head down, her eyes on her food. What she thought about Evan's offer was anyone's guess. Ian didn't want to know.

When Ian was seated as far from Mimi as he could get on the bench, Evan poked him with his plastic fork. "Scoot over, bench-hog. Don't think I'm sitting on the other side next to Betsy Wetsy."

Ian reluctantly slid closer to Mimi. Her leg, bared in her shorts, brushed against his. Her skin was soft. Warm. Ian clenched his can of soda, fingers putting dimples in the aluminum. He had two contradictory urges: the first, to stroke a hand over that smooth length, up to the hem of her shorts and beyond. The second, to stand up, take his plate of food to his wood shop and eat there in peace and safety. Mimi moved over a bit, but Jack needed some room on her other side. Their legs still touched with nothing to cool the building heat.

Meanwhile, the chatting and laughter flowed across the rough, unfinished boards of the table. Ian barely heard any of it. Evan kept leaning against him to grab the salt or taunt Anna with some barb. Ian knew his *friend* was using any excuse he could to push Ian against Mimi. Ian kept his hands on the table where he could see them, not trusting himself an inch. He barely tasted the ham sandwich he chewed; the potato salad might as well have been sawdust. All he smelled was Mimi's perfume and all he felt was her bare thigh softly pressing against his.

After the longest, most torturous twenty minutes in history, Ian got a reprieve. Jack finished his lunch and got up. Mimi immediately slid away from Ian, then jumped up from the table, too. She began clearing away empty plates without asking, as if she couldn't wait for the meal to end, either. Ian supposed that he ought to feel happy she found the situation as uncomfortable as he did, yet for some odd reason it ticked him off when she rushed to get away. *He* was the one who was keeping his distance. Not her. He stood and dumped his own plate in the trash. Mimi had a bottle of water in her hand, refilling Kate's glass. Ian took a last swig of soda and tossed his can into the recycle bin.

"I'm going back down to the boats," he announced to everyone.

"I'll come, too," Jack said.

"Not so fast, young man," Mimi said. "You've got schoolwork waiting at home."

"Mo-*om,* I've gotta stay and help Ian."

"Sorry, kiddo. I think you've played around enough for the day."

"But—" Jack's scowl appeared once more.

"No." Mimi's voice rang firm.

Though he knew he probably shouldn't say anything,

Ian couldn't help himself. "Come back next Saturday, runt. Class starts at ten."

"Really?" Jack's scowl cleared. "Great!"

"We'll see," Mimi said in a tight voice.

As childish as it was, her irritation made Ian feel better. He wasn't the only one leaving this meal unsettled. It also reminded him of his earlier annoyance with her. She was wrong and he wasn't going to back down from helping Jack. He smiled at her deliberately. "Nice seeing you, too, Mimi."

She glared at him, then turned to say goodbye to the rest of the crowd. "Thanks for lunch. Sorry we have to go."

Anna got up and gave her a hug. "I'll see you Monday."

"Yes, I can't wait to hear everything. Details," Mimi said with a grin. "I need details." Both women laughed and Mimi turned away. Herding Jack in front of her, she walked off without even glancing at Ian.

As Ian stood watching her go, Patrick came up beside him. "You know, we really ought to have her sign a permission and release form if you want Jack in the class."

"I'll get it. Later."

"What's going on between you two?"

Ian turned to his brother. "Nothing."

"Right."

Ian gave him the I-dare-you-to-contradict-me look that sometimes worked back when they were kids.

Patrick cocked his head a bit and looked at him for a long moment. Finally, he shrugged. "Have it your way, big brother."

Ian grunted and started back to the docks. Whatever Patrick thought, he was wrong. So was Mimi. If she wanted to fight over what was best for Jack, he was ready. He refused to think about what else he was ready to do with Mimi Green. Better to concentrate on Jack. Much better.

Chapter Five

When the doorbell rang, Mimi was almost ready. She raced out of her room to the top of the stairs. As she moved, she pushed a hank of hair behind her ear and quickly threaded a gold hoop earring into place. She rushed down the first flight of stairs. At the landing, she checked her lipstick in the mirror next to the coatrack.

"Just a second," she yelled to the shadow that lurked behind the stained glass at the front door.

A memory hit her as she skipped down the rest of the stairs. She had made this same mad dash many times in high school. She remembered always running late—hurrying through dressing, slapping on makeup—all in anticipation of going out on the town with friends. She flung the door open, a wide smile on her face.

"Am I running late or are you early?" she asked as she hugged Anna before tugging her inside.

"A little of both," Anna said with a smile.

Mimi laughed. "It's good to know some things don't change."

"This place still looks the same, too. I remember that picture."

Anna pointed to a sentimental painting of a heron fishing along some stretch of the Chesapeake shoreline. Mimi hardly noticed it; it had hung there in the entry for as long as she could remember. She bent and slipped her feet into strappy black sandals with low heels.

"I'm ready. At last."

Mimi followed Anna outside to the porch and into the heat. It hit like a blast from a furnace, the humidity adding an oppressive weight to the air. The sun was dazzling, and Mimi slipped her sunglasses on to shield against the glare. When they got in the car, Anna flipped the air-conditioning on high.

"Ugh, I forgot how awful summers are around here," Anna said as she backed out of the driveway.

"It's not so humid in California, is it? I played a few clubs in L.A. I loved it out there."

"I know it's supposed to be hotter there, but it never feels as bad as it does here."

"Admit it, you miss the heat, the humidity, the bugs."

"You forgot to mention my family." Anna shook her head and shot a glance at Mimi. "I don't know how you're doing it. Living with your parents, I mean."

"Lack of funds is my excuse," Mimi said with a chuckle. She paused, thinking of the past few months. "It's been good actually. Much better than I thought it would be. I guess ten years away has made me look at my parents differently. I like them. As people, I mean."

"And they don't interfere in your life?"

"Now, let's not slip into fantasy, girl."

They both laughed.

"They've been good for Jack, too," Mimi added. "It won't last much longer, though. Jack and I need to get our own place. I've been looking, and I think I'll be able to swing it by the time school starts in the fall."

Mimi asked about Anna's life in San Francisco and her career in architecture. Anna talked about the projects she was working on in California and collaborations with other firms in different cities scattered around the country. She had dated a variety of interesting men, but was still waiting for Mr. Right to knock on her door. Mimi felt in awe of her friend's success and her freedom. A bit jealous and humbled, too.

"What about you?" Anna asked. "Are you going to keep working at the bar?"

"I think so," Mimi said. "I've really enjoyed it this summer and my dad likes to have me there, too. I suppose someday I'll take over completely."

"And you can sing there whenever you want."

Mimi looked over at Anna, startled. "I haven't yet. I'm thinking about it," she said slowly.

Anna shot her a sharp look, then turned her attention back to the road. "Then where do you perform?"

"Nowhere. I'm done with that for a while."

"What?" Anna frowned. "Why?"

"It's a long story."

"So, get started. You said *you* wanted details? Well, right back at you."

Trying to keep it succinct, Mimi outlined the past ten years to her friend: the highs, the lows, the good times and the bad. She didn't dwell on the failures—always looming in her own mind—and skipped over her relationship with Jack's father. For Jack's sake, she was not ready to let Anna in on that secret. Anna asked a few questions, letting Mimi know that she understood what *wasn't* being said as well as what was. Before she could finish her story, Anna had pulled the car into an angled parking spot on a tree-shaded street. She let the car run to keep the air-conditioning and the conversation flowing.

"It sounds to me like you just need a sabbatical," Anna said. "Time off to regroup and figure out what comes next."

Mimi shrugged and opened her mouth to speak, but Anna

beat her to it. "You *can't* throw talent like yours away, Mim. You're too good. I still have that CD you sent me in college."

Mimi laughed, remembering that particular band. The music seemed so simple and derivative in retrospect. "That was almost eight years ago, Annie. Maybe I'm not as good as you remember."

Anna snorted. "Right. Talent like yours doesn't just fade over time, it gets better. Besides, I can't imagine you not playing and singing. It's who you are."

"Have you been talking to my dad?" Mimi asked, shaking her head.

"No, but I'm not surprised he thinks the same thing. I've always liked your father. He's a smart man, Mim. It's about time you started listening to him." She turned off the ignition and picked up her purse. "Come on. Let's go get lunch before we fry ourselves."

"Where are we going?"

"Celia's Garden. It's Kate's recommendation. She says the food is fantastic."

Both women got out of the car. Mimi followed her friend to a three-story brick building. The door was painted butter-yellow, the trim around it a vibrant turquoise. Stepping inside, they found themselves in a long narrow hallway with a high ceiling, the original passageway between two narrow row houses that had merged to make the restaurant. The walls on either side were painted to resemble a trellis with roses abounding. The floor was paved in square tan terrazzo tiles, adding to the gardenlike ambience.

"I wonder if there's a real garden back there somewhere," Mimi asked, craning her head to look up at the pink, white and red roses hanging from the ceiling.

At the end of the hall, the entrance opened up to a small waiting area with a hostess stand. Just then, the swinging doors in the back of the reception area parted and a tall bald man stepped forward to greet them.

"Welcome to Celia's. How *are* you?" he asked.

His tone made Mimi think he really cared about their well-being. She warmed to him immediately. His smile brought one to her lips.

"Hello. We're fine," Anna said. "How are you?"

"Oh, the heat! It's a killer." He put the back of one hand to his bald head. "And me with no natural protection to hide under. I'm just so grateful to be inside."

"We have a reservation. For Berzani," Anna said.

The man glanced at the book on the hostess stand. "Of course. I have a wonderful table for you. Come right this way." The man slipped two menus off a stack and led them up the stairs. At the top, he escorted them to a table at the front of the room, next to a window. Pulling out first one chair and then the other, he seated them with panache. When they were settled, he handed them each a menu, putting a third one on the table between them. He crossed his arms and tapped a finger on his chin.

"Now, the specials are inside your menus and these are the wines-by-the-glass." He patted the smaller folder on the table. "We have an extensive wine bar. If you want to see a full list, just let me know. I'll bring you some water and let you look over the menu. If you have any questions, don't hesitate to ask. My name is Christopher."

"Thanks, Christopher," Mimi and Anna said in unison. As he turned to go, their eyes met and both suppressed a giggle. Surely the waiter was putting on a performance for their amusement. But who could be sure?

Mimi looked around. The room was nearly full of diners, some in suits, some in jeans. There was an air of happy conviviality with cutlery and glassware clinking merrily. "Wow, this place certainly looks fabulous."

"Mmm." Anna picked up the wine list. "Want to splurge?"

"Definitely. This is our celebration."

Anna looked up. "Right. We have ten years to pay for."

Christopher returned promptly with two glasses of water, slices of lemon floating among the ice cubes. "Any questions so far?"

"We haven't even looked," Mimi said.

"Why bother? The specials are absolutely superb and our chef knows his way around a kitchen. Let me tell you about them." Christopher rattled off poetic, mouthwatering descriptions of four culinary masterpieces. "Take a moment to think those over. Read the menu if you don't trust me. I'll be back in a few."

The two looked at each other across the table and simultaneously set their menus aside. Anna picked up the wine list, then she passed it to Mimi. Without either one consulting the other, they both selected the pinot grigio. When Christopher returned again, they ordered it and their food. Mimi chose a vegetable pasta with pesto, while Anna opted for the spinach and Parmesan omelet. Shortly, he came back with the wine and set it down along with a basket of fragrant rolls of various shapes, sizes and colors. Two small pots of butter—one garlic, one herb—accompanied the tempting treats.

After he left them, Mimi picked up her glass of wine. "To old friends."

Anna raised her glass. "To friends at least. Speak for yourself about the old part."

Mimi laughed and tapped her glass against Anna's before sipping the cold, tart liquid. It was delightfully dry, with a hint of citrus. "I know it's been ten years since we've seen each other, but it seems like yesterday."

"For me, too. That's the best, isn't it?" Anna asked. "I don't have too many friends like that."

"I don't either. I suppose it's because I've moved around so much."

"But you're putting down roots now."

Mimi nodded, twirling the stem of her glass on the table. "Yes. As long as Jack's in school, this is home."

"How does that make you feel?"

"I have to do what's best for Jack."

"You've become a responsible parent."

"I know. It sounds so, so...*adult,* doesn't it?" Mimi wrinkled her nose as Anna laughed. "But it's what I want to do for him."

"When Ian introduced me to Jack, I couldn't believe he was yours," Anna said as she picked up her knife, scooped up butter and put it on her plate. "And that Johnny Sinclair is his father. That's even stranger."

Mimi's fingers clenched around the multigrain roll she had just picked up. "How did you know?"

"He looks just like him," Anna said, casually setting her knife and the bread on her plate. "He's got your eyes and hair, but his face is all Johnny."

Mimi put down the mashed roll and carefully wiped her hands on her napkin. Her stomach was clenched in a knot. Was it really so obvious? She hadn't thought so, but Anna had seen the resemblance right away. Of course, Anna had grown up with Johnny, just as Mimi had. She took a sip of wine, wondering how to handle this situation.

"I'm not supposed to know, am I?" Anna asked gently. She reached across the table to touch Mimi's hand.

Swallowing, Mimi raised her head. "I— Johnny's not Jack's father."

"It's okay, Mim. I won't tell anyone. You know that."

"I mean he *is* Jack's biological father, but that's it."

Her smile was merely a twist of her lips. "As it turned out, Johnny thought the idea of being a father was pretty strange, too."

Anna stared at Mimi for a long moment, then her face hardened. "He abandoned you? And his *baby?*"

"As he so eloquently put it, it wasn't his gig."

"I never liked Johnny, but I didn't think he was *that* much of a bastard."

Mimi shrugged and sipped her wine. "It worked out for the best, Annie. Johnny would have been a terrible father. At least he recognized that."

"I can't believe it! How could he just walk away and leave you alone with a child to raise?"

"And I've done a pretty good job, I think." This time Mimi laid her hand over Anna's. "I appreciate you feeling mad for me, but it was a long time ago."

"Then why did you get so upset that I knew he was Jack's dad?" Anna asked. "You went as white as this tablecloth." She thumped her finger on the crisp linen.

"I—" Mimi stopped and organized her thoughts for a moment. "No one but me and my parents know who Jack's dad is."

"Jack doesn't? Hasn't he asked?"

"No." Mimi shook her head, smoothing the napkin in her lap. "I keep expecting it, and I'll be honest if he asks, but he's never shown a bit of curiosity. I...I...have to admit that I'm not wild to tell him." She looked up at Anna. "I don't want him to be hurt because his father didn't want him. When he's older, maybe he'll be better able to understand."

"And Johnny's not just any old guy these days, is he? Having a rock star for a dad could be cool."

"Maybe, but I don't think nine is the age of reason when it comes to things like that. If Johnny weren't so famous, I might force the issue, but…" She let the words trail off. "I just want to be sure Jack's ready to handle it. You know?"

"Yes, I do know, Mim." Anna smiled. "It's a tough call, but it's yours. No one will hear about it from me."

"But you saw the resemblance right away." Mimi's stomach twisted again at the thought. "Who else might see it and *not* keep it a secret?"

Anna was silent as Christopher appeared at the table with two plates. With a flourish, he set the food before them and let the wonderful aromas waft under their noses. Mimi savored the crisp scent of basil and garlic as she admired the beautiful presentation of the pasta. Anna's omelet looked just as tasty, with cheese oozing out the edges.

"Now, can I get you beautiful ladies anything else?"

"Not right now," Anna said after sharing a smile with Mimi. "This should keep us in heaven for a while."

"Enjoy, then."

Both of them picked up their forks and began eating. After a few bites, Anna resumed their conversation.

"I wouldn't worry about anyone connecting Johnny and Jack," she said. "I think *I* did because I knew you and he were…involved."

Mimi chuckled. "That's one word for it."

Anna grinned. "Yeah, you were hot for each other." She took another bite of her omelet, chewed and swallowed. "Who else knew about you and Johnny?"

Mimi shook her head. "No one that I told. I didn't have any friends but you that I *would* tell. And Johnny didn't broadcast it."

"What a jerk," Anna said with a snort. "He probably wanted to preserve his playboy image."

"Exactly. I never caught on to that," Mimi said with a rueful laugh. "I *believed* him when he told me he wanted our relationship to be special, a secret just between us. I was *so* gullible."

"The man was all style and no heart. And you believed what you wanted to believe," Anna said with a shrug. "Thank goodness we only have to be seventeen for a year."

They both laughed, then Mimi sighed happily. "I have missed you so much. I can't believe we've let this much time go by without talking to each other."

"I know." Anna pushed her plate to one side. "After we graduated from high school, I couldn't wait to get away, go to college and start real life. In my rush to become an adult, I left a few good things behind me. You're one of them."

"Well, let's not let it happen again. The telephone is a wonderful invention that we should not neglect. And we can see each other when you come home."

"Crab Creek will never be home for me again."

Mimi raised her eyebrows at the ferocity of her friend's words. "Easy, girl. I'm not the one with the lasso and the branding iron."

"Sorry," Anna said ruefully. "I've been getting a lot of not-so-gentle hints that I should move back. My parents just don't get that I'm not like my siblings. I need my space."

"And you have a great career and a steady income. You've made your way in the big bad world. Your folks must be proud of you. You should try being a poor, starving musician who travels all the time *and* never comes to visit and had to call once or twice to ask for money. My mother *hated* what I loved to do," Mimi said with a laugh. "My dad was okay, though. He just wanted me to be happy."

Christopher came to remove their dishes and offer a dessert menu.

"What do you think? Chocolate?" Mimi asked.

"One of whatever's the most sinful and two forks," Anna said to the waiter. "You pick for us."

"You are an incredibly smart woman," Christopher said, giving Anna a light touch on the shoulder, then took the menu and their dishes away.

"So, you said living with your parents was okay, but are you happy?"

Mimi leaned forward, elbows on the table. "I think I'm *getting* to happy. It gets better, easier, every day."

"I don't know if I could come back and not feel like—" Anna abruptly cut herself short.

"A failure?" Mimi asked. Surprisingly, the word didn't hurt as much now as it had a few months ago.

"I didn't mean that—"

"It's okay." Mimi reached out at the same moment Anna did and their hands met and clung. "I *did* feel like a failure when I got back. Tail between my legs and nothing to show for ten years of reaching for the stars."

Anna turned her hand so that their fingers were linked. "You have a son you love, the support of your family and a future where anything is possible. That doesn't sound like *nothing* to me."

Tears sprang to Mimi's eyes. "Well, when you put it that way," she said with a wobbly smile as Anna pressed her fingers.

Dessert came and both women sat back. A slice of chocolate cake was placed in front of them. Whipped cream rose in a mound on one side, floating in a pool of raspberry-colored sauce. Fresh raspberries dotted the plate, some nestled in the cream with a sprig of mint just peeking out from underneath.

"Chocolate-raspberry torte," Christopher said. He laid two forks down, one on either side of the plate. "Dive in, ladies. I don't want to see one crumb left on that plate."

They didn't wait for another invitation. When the first bite started to melt on Mimi's tongue, she groaned. "This is wonderful."

Anna's hum of delight answered. "Better than sex."

"Well, maybe not *better*," Mimi countered with a wicked smile.

Anna looked up from the dessert and put a hand out as if to block Mimi's thoughts. "I do *not* want to hear any details about you and my brother. Eew," she said with a shudder.

Mimi froze, fork halfway to her mouth. "You think Ian and I are—"

"Stop." Anna's hand was still out. "Whatever's going on, keep it to yourself. Please."

Mimi carefully lowered her fork to the plate, her bite of cake still resting there. She knew she wouldn't be able to swallow if she tried. "I don't know where or how you came up with that silly idea, but—"

"I wasn't the only one who saw you two sitting together at lunch yesterday. The steam was so thick it was like being in a sauna."

"I barely know him!" Mimi's words stuttered to a stop, her voice strangled. "Plus, he's a total busybody, poking his nose in where it doesn't belong and telling me how to raise my son."

"Really?" Anna took another bite of cake, but somehow kept a saucy, knowing grin on her lips. "I had it all wrong, then."

Mimi felt a hot blush travel up her cheeks. "Yes, you did."

"Mimi's got a crush, Mimi's got a crush," Anna sang in a low, playground chant.

There was nothing to do but laugh at the childish taunt. Then Mimi blew out a breath and picked up her fork again, chewing and swallowing the bite of cake she had abandoned, hoping a burst of chocolate would straighten her fuddled thoughts. "I was such an idiot."

"Because you have the hots for Ian?" Anna licked whipped cream off her top lip. "*I* think it's weird, but he's my brother and I've known him a lot longer than you have."

"I do *not* have the hots for Ian or anyone else right now." Mimi took another bite. "No, I had a flashback to our sophomore year. Remember when we both had a crush on Bruce Croft? That's when I was an idiot."

"Bruce the Babe," Anna said with a sigh. "We were both idiots. To think our friendship almost broke up over those great-looking buns." She stuck her finger into the raspberry sauce and licked it off.

"Whatever happened to Bruce and his delightful buns?" Mimi wondered.

"He probably married Janey Murdoch and she fattened him up."

Mimi looked over at her friend for a long moment, then threw her head back and laughed. "I've missed you, Anna. I really have."

IAN TIGHTENED THE CLAMP carefully, aligning the door frame so the dovetailed joints in the corners were flush. After one more turn, he made sure the louvered slats were seated into place as the clamp closed. When it looked right, he checked the whole piece with a square and made a couple of small adjustments. He wiped off the excess glue where it had oozed from the joints, then racked the panel with three similar ones. Mopping his brow with his shirt-sleeve, he collected the pieces of teak he had already cut, and assembled the fifth door on his bench. Two more of these louvered cabinet doors and his portion of the refit would be finished. Then he could move on to the next job Patrick had posted on the schedule.

The door creaked open. Intent on applying glue to the joints, Ian barely glanced up. "No," he said to his brother.

"I haven't even asked you anything yet," Patrick complained.

"Yeah, but the only time you come in here is to load me up with more jobs."

"I'm hurt," Patrick said, pulling up a stool on the other side of the table.

"You'll get over it."

His brother was silent for a minute. "Listen, I was thinking—"

"Always a dangerous thing."

Patrick chuckled. "About this Saturday. I thought we could—"

The door opened again and Anna stepped inside. "Hey, guys."

"Why am I so popular today?" Ian muttered to himself.

"Hey, Annie. What's a girl like you doing in a wood shop like this?"

"Avoiding a mother and father who want to set me up on another date with a nice *local* boy." She set her purse on the workbench and leaned a hip against it. "Am I interrupting?"

"No," Patrick said.

"Yes," Ian countered almost as quickly. Ian saw Anna shoot a glance at Patrick.

"Sounds like somebody got up on the wrong side of the table saw," Anna teased.

"I've got two tons of work to do, thanks to Mr. Sure-we-can-have-it-done-by-next-week." Ian pointed a wooden slat first at Patrick, then at his sister. "And I don't need an audience."

"I could help," she offered.

Patrick snorted. "Right. Pretty architects should draw things. Not build them."

"You might be surprised. I know my way around a construction site."

"Like that tree house you helped me build?"

"I was seven years old." Anna crossed her arms over her chest and huffed out an irritated breath. "You're never going to let me live that down, are you? I've learned a few things about cantilevered loads since then, you know."

"I should hope so," Patrick said with a grin. "That thing came down in a hurry."

"Gravity is a merciless bitch," Ian added solemnly as he reached for another pipe clamp.

Patrick laughed. Ian saw Anna's eyes narrow to angry slits. He suddenly felt as though time had reversed and they were kids again. Anna had an Irish temper that matched all that bright red hair, and Patrick, like most older brothers, could never resist poking her.

"I think my degree and experience makes me better qualified to build things than you."

"It makes you qualified to tell people *how* to build things, maybe," Patrick said doubtfully.

Anna put her hands on her hips. Now her irritation was real. "Do you belittle Kate like this?"

"He wouldn't dare," Ian said, figuring it was time to referee—as usual—when the banter got too serious between them. "Better knock it off, Patty, before she whacks you with a plank."

"She started it," Patrick said in laughing protest. "Besides, teasing my baby sister just shows how much I miss her."

"How come you're so dressed up?" Ian asked Anna, trying to change the topic. "Got a hot date with one of Mom's preapproved matches?"

After one last warning glare at Patrick, Anna turned to Ian. "I went to lunch with Mimi."

Ian forced himself not to tense at the mention of the name. "Have a good time?"

"Fantastic! I've really missed her," Anna said. "I didn't realize how much until today."

"She's got a great kid," Patrick said.

A cell phone rang. Anna reached for her purse, but it was Patrick's. Looking at the screen, he rose from the stool. "Sorry, I've got to take this."

After Patrick stepped outside, Anna took his seat. "I really admire Mimi. She's sacrificed everything for her son. Don't you think?"

"Mmm." Ian kept his eyes on his hands as they fitted louvered slats into the slots of the frame. There was no way he was rising to whatever bait his sister was offering.

"She's even prettier than she was in high school, too."

"I didn't know her then," Ian said, hoping he sounded disinterested enough to make her give up her fishing expedition. No such luck.

"We talked about you."

"Great," Ian said in as neutral a tone as he could muster.

"She's definitely got the hots for you."

"She does?" His gaze flew up to meet his sister's. When he saw her eyes start to twinkle mischievously, Ian knew he was caught—hook, line and sinker.

"Gotcha," she said softly.

Ian looked back down at the wood frame in front of him. He closed his eyes briefly, then opened them. Fury rose in a wave. He slammed the block of wood he'd held down on the table. "Don't play games with me, Anna. This is not high school."

"I'm not playing games!"

"What do you call it then?" He leveled a hard look at her. "You waltz in here, spend a few hours with Mimi and start matchmaking. You're worse than Mom."

"I was just—"

"I'm leaving in exactly three months, seven days and eleven hours. I don't need any complications right now. I don't think your friend is interested in *that,* either."

Anna frowned at him, but remained silent. Finally, she nodded. "Okay. You've made your point."

"Good."

"I'm sorry, Ian."

"Yeah," he said softly. "Me, too." Her sad dark eyes told him she meant what she said. They also told him that she guessed just how deep his sorrow went. He lowered his head and pretended to look at the pieces of wood on the bench. "I need to finish this panel."

"Sure." She fidgeted with her purse handle, then picked it up and stood. "Well, I guess I better go. I'll see you at dinner?"

"If Dad's at the grill, I'm there," Ian answered with a half smile.

She left without another word and Ian heard the door click behind her. He stood quietly, his hands on the bench, waiting for his mind to clear. His eyes automatically traced the shape of the frame he had just assembled, soothing his thoughts. Suddenly, he noticed that something was wrong. He had reversed two of the louvers.

Shaking his head, he undid the clamps, but the glue had already set. He would have to cut all the wood for it again. What a waste—a stupid, boneheaded mistake. A burst of impatient anger streaked through him. Ian cursed and threw the frame across the room. It hit the far wall and split into a dozen pieces. Running his hand over his head and back to his neck, he massaged a knot there that would not budge. He had made too many mistakes to be sorry about lately. Meeting Mimi Green was at the top of the list.

Chapter Six

Mimi shifted in her seat, gripped the black leather purse in her lap and wished she could get up to pace. Jack sat at her side staring at the floor. One of his legs swung back and forth, bumping against the chair leg. Mimi put a hand on his knee. He flashed her a glance and she gave one brief shake of her head. His leg stopped moving, but he started to pick at the armrest of the chair instead. A mother and daughter came out of the principal's office, the mother with a determined grimace, the young girl's head downcast.

"Mr. James will see you now, Ms. Green," the secretary said.

Mimi rose, smoothing down the skirt of her navy dress. Borrowed from her mother, she hoped the outfit made her look serious and mature. She had scooped her hair back into a neat French twist and added pearl earrings to complete the ensemble. Still, she was nervous, as if she had done something wrong for which the principal would punish her.

Jack had jumped to his feet, too, only to sink back into his chair with a scowl when the secretary asked Mimi to go in alone. Mimi put her hand under Jack's chin and tilted his head up so their eyes met. "Behave," she said softly.

Jack shrugged and squirmed away from her touch. Mimi

turned and opened the door to the inner office. From behind a desk, a tall, portly man rose and extended his hand.

"Ms. Green. It's nice to see you again," he said, shaking her hand and closing the door behind her. "Please, have a seat."

Mimi sat facing his broad desk while the principal took the chair behind it. She had been here once before, when she had enrolled Jack in school after their return to Crab Creek. From that visit, she had come away liking the man who oversaw the school; he seemed genuinely interested in educating her son.

Mr. James glanced at some reports in a file on his desk and frowned slightly, then folded his hands, one over the other, on his desk. "Ms. Green, I asked you to come in today with Jack to discuss his progress in our school."

"I'm happy you've taken an interest in him."

"Ms. Green, do you get a chance to supervise his homework?"

"Yes, I've been working with him as much as I can. It's been a struggle, but I think he's improving." Mimi's voice rose on a hopeful note. "His grandfather has been helping him with numbers, too, and Jack's score on his last math test was better."

"I saw that in his teacher's report," Mr. James said. His tone told Mimi he wasn't nearly as hopeful.

"I know he's not quite caught up on his English assignments, but I promise you, he'll get them done this week."

"I'm sure Ms. Scheuer will be glad to hear that." The principal paused. His eyes were kind, though his face was solemn. "Jack is at the bottom of his class, Ms. Green. And despite your efforts at home, his performance has slipped even further these past two weeks," Mr. James said gently. "I must tell you that, as it looks right now, we cannot pass Jack to fifth grade."

Mimi sucked in a sharp breath. The words struck with the force of a blow, sending her thoughts reeling. She tried to focus on the man sitting opposite, but her vision was hazy for a moment. "What? Are you sure?"

Mr. James flipped through some papers. "Unfortunately, yes. Jack is struggling to keep up with his peers. He always seems to be just on the edge of failing. Not only at this school, either. I've looked at the records from his previous schools this year and I see the same pattern."

"But he did the extra homework," Mimi said urgently. "He brought his grades up."

"In *this* school, yes, he has," Mr. James said with a nod. "But the transcripts from his other schools tell a different story. I'm afraid that if he goes on to fifth grade, he'll just fall further and further behind." Mr. James continued citing data from the pages in his file to prove his point.

Mimi held up a shaking hand to stop him. "How is it that I'm hearing about this on the last week of school?"

"I do apologize for that, but please understand that your son hasn't been a student here long. It took a while to get all Jack's transcripts transferred, and for me and his teacher to evaluate them," Mr. James said. "As you know, your son's schooling has been…shall we say, varied."

That pause was like a lash on Mimi's back. "We've moved around a lot," she said, her voice shrill in her own ears.

"Yes. I can see that."

A flush of heat rose in her cheeks and a wave of panic threatened to overwhelm her. She dug her fingers into the leather of her purse and tried to stay calm. "Mr. James, if Jack has to repeat fourth grade I'm afraid he'll get too discouraged and he'll give up altogether."

"Yes, I'm concerned about that possibility, too. So,

before we take that drastic of a step, I'd like us to try another alternative."

"Which is?"

"Enroll Jack in summer school, starting next week. We have an excellent program. *If* he applies himself, I believe he can catch up to the rest of the students in his class by the end of the summer."

"Of course," Mimi said. She needed no time to make the decision. "Tell me when and where and I'll make sure he's there every day."

Mr. James folded his hands again as he looked over at her. He cleared his throat and smiled. "Jack is a bright boy, Ms. Green."

"Not so bright that he isn't failing school," Mimi said with a wry twist to her lips.

The principal chuckled a little. "No, that's true." He looked down and then back at Mimi, his face serious. "I spent quite a bit of time going over Jack's records and reading the evaluations his past teachers have written. I also had Jack tested recently."

"Tested?"

"Standard evaluations. Nothing out of the ordinary. But, Ms. Green, your son is *very* bright," Mr. James said.

"That's good, isn't it?" Mimi cocked her head to the side a little, wondering where this conversation was going.

"It is," he agreed. "I really think Jack's intelligence is what has kept him from failing before. The number of schools the boy has attended? It's not surprising that he's behind in his classes. It also explains why he has difficulty making friends and fitting in socially."

Nausea washed over Mimi. She gritted her teeth together against it. Every word the principal said was like an ax chopping down the life she and Jack had lived. "He won't be moving from now on," she said. "We're here to stay."

"That will be good for Jack, certainly," Mr. James said with a nod. "But what I'm trying to say is that just being sure Jack attends school won't be enough. Somehow, we have to convince him to learn."

"Of *course* he'll learn. I'll make sure—"

Mr. James held up a hand, patting the air as if to calm her. "We can all tell Jack to do the schoolwork, we can stand over him and watch him do it, but unless we capture his interest, he will continue to just skate through. Ms. Green, I think a significant portion of Jack's problem is boredom. Because he is bored, he doesn't pay attention. Because he doesn't pay attention, he fails. When he fails, he thinks school is a waste of time and he gets more bored with it. It's a spiraling circle down."

"So what do I do?"

"Getting him in to the summer school program will be a start. The teacher this year is very good at challenging her students. I've already spoken to her so she is aware of Jack's situation."

"Thank you."

Mr. James leaned forward in his chair. "We need to find a way to capture Jack's attention, some incentive. Is there something that motivates him? Something you can reward him with if he applies himself? Is he into some particular sport or activity?"

"Well, he likes music. And he's recently become interested in sailing."

"There you go." Mr. James held up his hands as if all their problems were solved.

Mimi remembered her argument with Ian Berzani about Jack's education. To her chagrin, the principal seemed to be agreeing with him. She looked down at her purse and noticed the marks her nails had made in the leather. Loosening her grip, she looked back at the principal. "So if he pays attention in school and does the work, I should reward him with something he likes."

"Exactly. Sometimes, it's that simple."

"He's going to hate going to school in the summer."

Mr. James smiled, a twinkle in his eyes. "*That* is a foregone conclusion. I've never had one child who didn't. But if he profits from it, it's worth the pain." The principal sat back in his chair. "Let's bring Jack in here and talk to him about it. I'm sure he's anticipating the worst, as it is."

Mimi agreed and steeled herself for the coming battle.

HALF AN HOUR LATER, Mimi and Jack walked out of the school to their car. Jack was quiet, his hair down over his eyes like a shield. Inside the car, Mimi paused before starting the engine.

"I guess we have some work to do."

Jack remained obdurately silent, his face turned toward the window. Mimi reached out and brushed a hand over his head, but he ducked away. Her heart aching, she turned the key and drove them home. Jack kept his face averted for the entire trip, then dashed out of the car and into the house without waiting for her.

Inside, Claire and George waited anxiously. "How did it go?" Claire asked quietly.

In a few brief sentences, Mimi told them what had happened and what had been decided. "So, here we are," she finished with a sigh, sitting down at the kitchen table across from her parents.

Claire put her hand over her daughter's and patted it gently. "If summer school is what it takes to get him on track, that's what he'll do."

Mimi turned her hand so that their fingers interlaced. "Think you could convince Jack of that?" She shook her head. "He thinks it's my fault that he has to go. In a way, I guess he's right."

"You are not to blame for this, Mim," her father said sternly.

"Aren't I?" Mimi looked at her parents. She felt tears begin to well up in her eyes, but blinked them away quickly. Holding up a hand to stop whatever they were about to say, she forced a smile to her lips. "Don't answer that. This isn't about me right now. I have to focus on Jack."

Her parents were silent, then her father asked, "So how do we convince him to go to school?"

Mimi grimaced. She had come up with an answer to that question on the drive home, but she didn't like it now any more than she had then. "I go talk to Ian."

"What for?" George asked.

"He's got the carrot that will lure Jack," Mimi said. "After Saturday, I think Jack would do just about anything to get on a sailboat again. Even go to school in the summer."

"Well, that's perfect then," Claire said with a relieved smile. "I'm sure Ian will do whatever he can, dear. He's a very nice man."

Mimi looked at her mother, opened her mouth, then closed it. *Nice* was not a word that would stick to Ian Berzani. "We'll see. I'll hope you're right." With that, Mimi rose and went to the door. "Wish me luck."

Outside, forcing herself forward, Mimi walked slowly down the street to A&E Marine, postponing a meeting with Ian. She was going to have to grovel, and the prospect was not a happy one. As usual for a hot summer day, the yard was busy. She looked around the stacked boats, but saw neither Ian nor Patrick. A sign pointed to the office, so she turned to go there.

As she crossed the parking lot, she spied a too-familiar

backside climbing down a ladder a few boats down. She reached the boat just as Ian stepped off the bottom rung. Standing right behind him, Mimi swallowed the lump in her throat. Before she could speak, Ian swung around. When he saw her he jumped, the tool bag in his hand dropping to the ground with a clang and clatter.

"Holy shit!" Ian stumbled back against the ladder, hitting his head.

Mimi lunged forward, hands outstretched. "I'm sorry. I didn't mean to startle you."

"What the hell are you doing?" he said in a growl. He avoided her touch, pushing himself away from the aluminum steps and rubbing the back of his head.

"Are you all right?" Mimi asked, taking a hasty step backward.

"I'm fine." Ian reached down for his tool bag, picking up a couple of chisels that had jumped out of it.

"I just…I need to talk to you."

Standing up, he glared down at her. "About what?"

Mimi stiffened at his scathing tone. "I'm sorry I frightened you—"

"You didn't *frighten* me. What do you want?"

Irritation flashed through Mimi. She wanted to turn and walk away, but she had to do this for Jack's sake. "I'm sorry I got annoyed with you about Jack last Saturday. I was wrong and you were right. He needs to learn to sail."

At her first words, Ian stilled. His eyes narrowed as he listened. "So?"

"I should have known this would be impossible," Mimi said with an exasperated sigh. "Forget it. Just *forget* it."

She turned to stomp away, but Ian caught her arm. "Hold on a minute. Forget what?"

Mimi gave him the short version of the meeting with the

principal. "So he—*I* think that the best way to entice Jack is to offer him sailing as a reward for summer school."

"And if he doesn't toe the line, you want me to punish him by not letting him sail."

"It's supposed to be a reward. Not a punishment."

"It cuts both ways, Mimi," Ian said, his eyes hard. "What are you going to do if his grades aren't any better now than before?"

Mimi fumed. Why was he making this more difficult than it had to be? "I'll deal with that when I have to. I just want to know if you'll help me."

Ian was silent, watching her with enigmatic eyes. Finally, he nodded. "Yeah, I'll help Jack."

Though she should feel grateful, Mimi had the urge to smack him. He had made it clear: he was doing this for her son, not for her. "Thanks. That's all I needed to know."

With that, she turned on her heel and walked away from him. In a way, she was glad he had behaved so badly. It reminded her of just what a jerk he had turned out to be. Sure he had a body to die for, but his personality and manners left a whole lot to be desired. If it wasn't for Jack, Ian Berzani could go to hell and she would help him get there.

MIMI SLOSHED TWO PINT GLASSES into the sudsy water, then rinsed them before plunging them into the disinfectant and setting them on the drain board. She looked around the bar for more chores to do: dusting the bottles, restocking refrigerators, refilling condiment dishes, anything. There was nothing to do. The tables were clean, the bar sparkled and every one of her ten customers had full glasses in front of them. With a sigh, she wiped her hands on a bar towel and leaned against the back counter.

The past three days had been miserable. Jack wasn't

speaking to her—or anyone. Ever since their meeting with the principal he had been sullen, silent and remote. Not even his grandfather could pull a smile out of him. He refused to go to summer school on any terms. Mimi had tried to soothe him, to coax him, but even the possibility of sailing school on Saturday was no enticement. In the end, she had told Jack the harsh truth: he was going whether he wanted to or not. From then on, he gave her the silent treatment.

The door swung open and Mimi perked up, expecting a customer. She slumped back when she saw her father enter the bar. He walked around the counter and patted her on the shoulder.

"How's it going?"

"Slow."

He looked at her from beneath shaggy eyebrows. "And my grandson? Still mad at the world?"

"Is the sky still blue?"

"He'll get over it."

"In my lifetime?" Mimi muttered.

George chuckled. "Why don't you get out of here for a while?"

"And do what?" Mimi asked morosely.

"Go practice your guitar so you can sing tomorrow night."

"What! Are you crazy?"

"Do it for Jack. It will pull him out of the dumps, don't you think? He was pretty excited by the idea when we first talked about it."

A thread of hope and anticipation began to weave around Mimi, though she tried to reject it. "You think it's that simple," she said, shaking her head.

"I do. So much so, that I already printed these."

George handed her a flyer that announced, "Mimi Green

returns to the stage! An intimate, unplugged performance at the Laughing Gull Tavern." It had the usual raves snipped from reviews of her past performances.

"I can't believe you did this!" Mimi wasn't sure if she was pleased or upset.

George smiled. "The job of Mimi Green's publicity agent was vacant, so I applied for the position and hired myself."

"Don't you think you should have asked me first?"

"No. This saves time. You would have wasted a good hour arguing with me when you should be practicing."

Mimi shook the handbill at her father. "I might need more than twenty-four hours to get ready, you know."

George dismissed her complaint with a wave of his hand. "That's plenty of time for a pro like you."

As Mimi thought about the best way to fire her new publicity agent, the front door swung open again and Anna walked inside.

"Well, Anna Berzani," George said with a wide smile as he stepped out from behind the bar and gave her a hug. "I'd have recognized that red hair anywhere."

"Mr. Green! How are you?" Anna pulled back and tugged on a lock of her hair. "Hasn't gotten any darker, has it? I don't know *why* I believed my mother when she said it would. Hers is exactly the same color."

Mimi and George both laughed at Anna's obvious disgust.

"What's up?" Mimi asked. "I thought you were going to Patrick and Kate's house tonight."

"I am," Anna said, slipping onto a stool. "But I need some fortification before I go. I just found out that Mom convinced Patty to invite one or two of his sailing buddies. Single ones."

"She *is* persistent, isn't she?" Mimi said with a chuckle.

"That's one way to put it," Anna said with a sigh, one elbow leaning on the bar. "Oh, well. Two more days and I'm out of here. I think I can manage to fend off engagement rings for that long."

"Fortification coming right up," George said. "What'll it be, ma'am?"

Anna smiled and sat up straight. "Ooh, a serious adult beverage. How about a margarita?"

"Coming right up. Mim, you joining her?"

"Yeah," Mimi said with a smile, coming around the bar to sit on the stool next to her friend. "I need at *least* one."

"You let her drink on the job?" Anna asked, raising an eyebrow at George.

"She's off the clock," he said, deftly pouring tequila and Triple Sec, then adding mixer. "She's supposed to be practicing for her gig here tomorrow night."

"You're playing?" Anna asked excitedly. "What time?"

"Nine o'clock." George set the two salted glasses on the bar and gave Anna a few handbills. "Invite everyone you know."

"This is exciting," Anna said. She picked up her glass. "To Crab Creek's newest singing sensation."

"Whoever he or she may be," Mimi said dryly, and they clinked glasses.

George moved down the bar to serve another customer and Anna turned to Mimi. "What brought this on? I thought you retired from the stage."

Mimi took a sip of the margarita. The salt was perfect with the tang of the lime. "Don't ask me. It's Dad's idea. I just heard the news myself right before you came." She twisted the glass around on the coaster. "He thinks I need a push."

"I agree with him."

"You would." Mimi used the stir stick to poke at the ice in her glass. "He also thinks it will help Jack."

"What's wrong with Jack?"

"He and I had a chat with his principal on Tuesday."

"And?" Anna prompted after Mimi remained silent for a long time.

"He isn't going to pass fourth grade." Mimi put her hands over her face. She couldn't hold back the tears this time. "God, I am such a failure."

"Oh, Mimi. Don't be ridiculous. You are not!" Anna handed her a cocktail napkin.

In a muffled voice, Mimi recounted her meeting with Jack's principal, her short conversation with Ian and how Jack refused to budge in spite of her best efforts. With a sniff, she looked over at her friend. "So, there you go. More fallout from me chasing dreams."

"Maybe. It sounds fixable to me, though," Anna said. They sipped in silence for a while. "At least this explains Ian's foul mood."

Mimi raised her head. "What are you talking about?"

"Big brother's been in a snit for days, but he wouldn't say why." Anna took a drink.

"Anna, I have to tell you that your brother is an arrogant *jerk*," Mimi said vehemently.

"Really? Ian?" Anna frowned. "Arrogant and jerk don't sound like him. Patrick, on the other hand, yeah, but Ian's much too down-to-earth."

"Trust me," Mimi said. "I could have smacked him."

"You should have. He probably deserved it," Anna said with a laugh. She looked at her watch and lifted her drink.

"This has been wonderful, but I've got to go ward off more potential suitors."

"Thanks for letting me cry on your shoulder."

"It was my pleasure." Anna stood and hugged Mimi. She grabbed the handbills George had given her earlier. "Save me a table for tomorrow night. I will definitely be here."

Anna thanked George for the margarita and left. Mimi sat where she was and looked at one of the flyers. *Tomorrow night*. The anticipation began to build again. She spun off her stool and headed for the door. She had some practicing to do. Funny how the prospect of singing made her feel alive and full of hope in an otherwise hopeless week.

Chapter Seven

"Hey, Ian, where's your little worker?" Evan asked as he, Patrick and Ian laid out masts, sails and rigging next to the eleven Optimists arranged on the dock. "We could use the help."

Ian shrugged. "Ask his mother."

"Oh? I thought you had that base covered," Evan said slyly. "Maybe I'll have to step in and try my luck again."

"Stow it, McKenzie."

Evan laughed, unperturbed until he caught sight of ten excited children coming their way. "Here we go again," he muttered.

Ian followed his gaze; for once, he agreed with Evan. He was in no mood to teach sailing. Yet shrieks of laughter and shouts of glee quickly surrounded the three men. Patrick soon had all the students rigging their dinghies. As he helped two boys untangle the wires, rope and sails from their mast, Ian kept glancing up the dock, looking for Jack. There was still no sign of him when the first Optimist launched. By the time the tenth went in the water, Ian was fuming.

Whenever Ian had thought about Mimi Green this past week, aggravation rose. Their encounters—her stubbornness—exasperated him. His clumsy, embarrassing reaction to the unexpected sight of her had only compounded his annoyance. As a further reminder, the lump on his head from the ladder was still there. Tuesday, she had asked for assistance he couldn't refuse to give. Today, she had kept Jack at home, no doubt to punish the kid. It was the wrong way to go about it, but experience told him she wouldn't listen to sense.

Once the fleet was under way—minus one red-and-yellow-striped sail—Ian jumped into a powerboat. The breeze was brisk enough that he, Patrick and Evan all needed to be out on the water. The two hours flew as Ian called instructions and corralled boats that strayed too far from the herd. Soon, all ten skippers and dinghies were tied to the dock again. Ian helped stow the boats, life jackets, sails and other gear, including the stuff he had laid out for Jack. After the last parent had picked up the last kid, Ian was still seething.

Patrick grabbed the box of bottled water they had brought down for the students. "Anyone want one of these?"

"I'd rather have a beer," Evan said, falling into step beside Ian as he walked up the pier. "I've earned at least one."

"Me, too," Patrick said. "Who'd have thought that teaching kids to sail would be so exhausting?"

"Remind me again—why did I agree to do this?" Evan asked.

"You were probably drunk at the time," Ian said dryly.

"Definitely." Evan shook his head.

"Hey, Jack," Patrick called suddenly. "You're late."

Ian followed his brother's gaze to the shore. Jack stood there in the mud, stick in one hand, his face set. Even at this distance, Ian sensed unhappiness radiating from his thin body.

"Hey, kid," Evan said. "You forget to set your alarm clock?"

Ian shot a glance at the other two men. "I'll catch up to you guys later," he said and grabbed two bottles from the box that Patrick carried.

"Sounds good," Patrick said easily.

Jack ducked his head and looked away as the men passed over the ramp near him. Ian turned and walked through the reeds to where Jack stood. He pushed his sunglasses to the top of his head so he could meet the boy, eye to eye. "Hey, what's up?"

"Nothing."

"Let's take a walk."

Jack shrugged and tossed his stick into the water. Silently, Ian led the way back down the dock, glancing covertly to make sure Jack followed. The boy kept his face averted, hair hiding his eyes. At the end of the pier, Ian sat on a dock box. From here, they could see the open water of the Chesapeake Bay. A few sails off in the distance hardly seemed to move, especially compared to the powerboats that buzzed back and forth like sports cars.

The boy sat down, his feet dangling above the dock. Ian cracked open a bottle of water and handed it to him. Jack sipped from it, his eyes on the boats. Ian unscrewed the cap on his own bottle and chugged half the contents. He let the silence between them linger for a while as they both took in the view.

"So. Why'd you skip class this morning?" Ian looked over at Jack, eyes narrowed in the bright sunlight.

The abrupt question seemed to startle Jack. He dropped the plastic bottle. Water gurgled out to form a puddle as he put his hands up to cover his face. At the first sob, Ian slid closer and put a tentative hand on one thin shoulder. Immediately, he found himself with an armful of crying boy.

"Hey, now. It can't be that bad," he said gently as

he rubbed Jack's back in slow, soothing circles. "What happened?"

The boy could not—or would not—answer. The pain that gushed out in great sobs was too enormous for his small bones. Ian waited patiently for it to recede, keeping his arms around Jack. As he sat, he looked out over the water again. A Chesapeake Bay deadrise had wandered into the creek, its diesel engines throbbing in a low-voiced roar. Small pink-and-green-striped buoys floating in the creek marked the position of the waterman's traps. He plucked the first from the water with his boat hook, then wrapped the rope around a pulley attached to the side of the craft. When the trap cleared the water, the waterman rested it on the gunnel and yanked open the top. He pulled out three crabs, kept one and tossed the other two back, put in fresh bait and dropped the whole thing over the side. Then he gunned the engine and spun over to the next buoy.

By the time the ninth trap was emptied and freshly baited, Jack's crying had eased. Ian could feel the small body slowly relax. When Jack finally sat up, Ian handed him a faded bandanna from his pocket. The boy blew his nose while Ian picked up the bottle. There were still a few swigs left. After wiping his eyes on the sleeves of his T-shirt, Jack took the bottle and drank.

"Did your mom tell you not to come to class?" Ian asked.

"No," Jack said. His voice was slightly nasal. Wiping his eyes again, he looked over at Ian. His lashes were spiked and wet, his cheeks flushed.

"So why didn't you come?"

"I didn't think you'd want me here."

Ian frowned. "Where'd you get that idea?"

Jack's shoulders sagged. He crushed the empty plastic bottle in his hands. "'Cause I'm a dummy."

"No you're not, runt." Sensing where this was going, Ian put a hand on Jack's shoulder and gave him a little shake. "You have dumb ideas like that sometimes, but *you're* not dumb."

"The principal says I am."

Ian's heart ached. "That's pretty harsh. Did he *really* say that?"

Jack shrugged, silent. "I flunked," he mumbled, then glanced at Ian, a defiant, lightning flash of blue.

"That's too bad." Ian squeezed Jack's shoulder.

"He says I have to go to summer school," Jack said in a rush. "My mom said she'd *make* me. And I can't come sailing if I don't." He squeezed the plastic bottle he held even tighter.

"So that's why you didn't come to class? To get back at your mom?"

The boy didn't look at him. "She doesn't care about me. She just tells me what to do and I have to do it."

"Your mom cares about you, runt."

"Then how come she's making me go to school?" The boy looked at Ian, his blue eyes full of anger and anguish in equal parts. "All *summer.*"

Ian took a deep drink of his water, wishing it were something a whole lot stronger. He sighed. "You know, *my* mom made me go to summer school once."

"Really?" Jack squinted at Ian skeptically.

"Yep. Except it was in seventh grade. I flunked English and history. Mostly because I'd farted off all semester." He looked over at the boy, one eyebrow raised. Jack squirmed, but remained silent. "She made me quit the baseball team until my grades got better, too."

"Your mom's mean. Like mine."

"Sometimes she is," Ian agreed with a laugh. "I sure was mad at her, but she didn't budge an inch. She told me that she loved me and that she wanted the best for me. If I thought that was mean, she didn't care. You know what?" Ian held Jack's gaze with his own. "She was right and I was wrong."

The boy absorbed the information and was silent for a long time. "I hate school," he finally declared.

Ian chuckled. "Yeah. I did, too, runt." Seeing the boy's unhappiness return, Ian got to his feet. "Come on. I want to show you something."

"You gonna make me work?"

"Only if you want to."

Jack bounced up and they walked down the dock, then turned left onto a side pier that led to deeper water. When they reached a white-hulled cutter, Ian stopped.

"Well, what do you think?"

"It looks like a big sailboat."

"See, you're not so dumb." He scrubbed a hand over Jack's head, making him giggle. "She's mine, all thirty-six feet of her."

"Wow! Really? Can I get on it?" Jack's eyes were wide as he took in the sturdy sailboat.

"She's not an *it*. All boats, at least the ones that someone loves, are *she*. Her name's *Minerva*. And, yes, you can get on her."

Agile as a monkey, the boy climbed up over the lifelines and onto the deck. In seconds he was standing on the cabin top.

"You could use the boarding step," Ian said with a laugh. Moving to the center of the boat, he did just that. On deck, he studied Jack's face. "So, what do you think?"

"This is so cool! She's big. Did you build her?"

"Mostly. When I bought her, she was nothing but a fiberglass hull and deck. It took me about four years to finish her."

"How fast can she go?"

"Not as fast as one of Patrick's racers, but fast enough."

Jack climbed all over *Minerva,* asking questions. Ian couldn't help feeling a bit of pride as he showed Jack how the cutter was rigged, how the self-steering vane worked and how the solar panels generated electricity for lights and refrigeration. The boat was his life's ambition. Now all he lacked was the opportunity to take her to sea and chase the setting sun.

"Can we go sail it sometime?" Jack asked as he stood behind the wheel, turning the rudder to port, then starboard.

"Maybe. It depends."

"On what?"

"How well you do in summer school."

Jack stopped playing with the wheel and peered warily at Ian. "What do you mean?"

"Your mom says you can't take sailing lessons unless you go to summer school, right?" At the boy's nod, he continued. "Well, I've got a deal for you, too. You *work* in school and I'll take you sailing on *Minerva.*"

"How many times?"

"We'll go once a week, as long as I see progress. No farting around," Ian added with a stern look.

Jack frowned as he considered the offer. Perched as he was on the seat, his gaze was nearly level with Ian's, who was standing in the well of the cockpit. Their eyes met and held. Ian could practically hear the gears turning in Jack's head.

Ian held out his hand. "Deal?"

Lower lip protruding, the boy huffed a sigh that blew his hair out of his eyes. "I still get to sail the little boats?" he asked cautiously.

"There's one for you as long as you keep up your end of the bargain with your mother. But that's between you and her," Ian said. He patted a hand on the dodger. "Learn to sail on them and you'll be able to handle *Minerva,* or any boat, after that."

"When can we go out on this one?"

"Tomorrow afternoon."

"Deal!" Jack thrust his hand into Ian's.

"Of course, we have to clear it with your mom," Ian said. Jack ducked his head and Ian had a suspicious thought. "She knows where you are, doesn't she?"

The boy shrugged. "I don't know. Maybe."

With a sigh, Ian pointed Jack to the steps. "Let's go, runt."

They made their way back to shore and through the yard. As they reached the main gate, Ian saw Mimi hurrying down the sidewalk. Her face was tense with concern. She caught sight of them and stopped for a second, then continued until she was hugging Jack fiercely.

"This is the second time you've scared me to death!" she said, pulling back and bending to catch his eyes. "Don't you ever do that again."

"Jack was just on his way home," Ian said, defending the boy and himself, too. Mimi's hair swirled around her face, her eyes a deeper blue from her anguish. Was that how they looked when she was aroused? He shoved the idea away as if it were on fire.

Still gripping Jack's shoulders, she looked up at Ian. "Thank you for taking care of him."

Ian shrugged and stuck his hands in his pockets, keeping himself from reaching out and taking her in his arms. Where was the irritation he had felt earlier? All he wanted now was to comfort her, soothe her the way he had just soothed her son. But if he took her in his arms, he wasn't sure he could keep from kissing her. Once he started doing that, it might never end.

"Me'n Ian made a deal," Jack announced.

Mimi looked at her son, frowning slightly. "What kind of deal?"

"If I work hard at summer school," Jack said, his face alight with a smile, "Ian's going to take me sailing on his boat."

"His boat?" Her shoulders stiffened and she shot Ian a glance. He couldn't tell if she was pleased by the idea or furious.

"I'm gonna go tell Grandpop," Jack said, then dashed away down the sidewalk, headed for the Laughing Gull.

"I can't believe it," Mimi said softly as she watched him run.

She ran a hand through her hair, pushing it back from her face, and blew out a breath. Ian's fingers itched to stroke the silky mass for himself. When she turned back to face him, he was shocked to see the sparkle of tears in her eyes. Before he could stop them, Ian's hands were out of his pockets and cupping her shoulders. She felt small and fragile under his palms.

"I'm sorry," she murmured, wiping the wetness away with a hand that shook. "It's just been a horrible week."

"It's okay," he said, his voice a low rumble.

Her gaze wouldn't meet his, staying fastened to the faded A&E marine logo on his T-shirt. Ian's heart nearly stopped when she reached out and traced the letters with one finger.

"He hasn't spoken to me in days. Yet you get him to go to school and be happy about it." She flashed him a glance, then looked down again. "I should be relieved, but I…I'm jealous, I guess."

"Sorry. I didn't—"

"No. Don't apologize. I should be the one doing that. Again," she finished on a sigh.

Ian was at a loss for words. When she took a step closer and rested her head on his shoulder, he froze. Seconds later, instinct took over and he slid his arms around her. Her scent—delicate, floral and intoxicating—filled his head as she settled against him. He could feel her breath in warm gusts against his neck. He could feel his own heart galloping. Surely, she must hear it, too.

Her hands gripped his biceps, her breasts just pressing into his chest. He felt her shiver in his arms as she took a gulped breath. *She was crying!* He closed his eyes, wishing he knew what to do. Holding her lightly, Ian stroked a hand over her back, much as he had done for her son. He tried to keep his touch comforting, tried *not* to think about raising her chin and kissing her soft lips. His teeth clamped together with the Herculean effort to leash his desire. When she pulled back moments later and he let his arms fall away, a wave of regret ran through him. She had felt good in his arms, right.

"I *am* sorry," she said, still not looking at him.

"For what?"

She brushed a hand across her eyes again. "For tangling you up in my mess."

Ian saw a blush color her cheeks. "I don't mind. I like Jack." He winced at his lame comment. Somehow, this woman tied his tongue in knots.

Mimi sucked in a breath as she took another step away from him. "So. Jack gets to sail with you. That sounds great. He's obviously excited. And he agreed to go to summer school? That's amazing. Really. I'll just—" For a moment, she seemed tongue-tied herself. She flipped a hand down the street toward the Gull. "I'll see you later."

With that, she turned around and walked away. Confused,

Ian watched her leave, his eyes lingering on her swaying hips. His mouth grew dry. She had the sweetest bottom he had seen in a long time—maybe his whole life. Her legs, bared in a short skirt, were luscious, and he could imagine them wrapped around his waist as he— Suddenly, she turned around and walked back to him. Ian bit the inside of his mouth and braced himself, hands shoved firmly back in his pockets. She put her hands on his shoulders and kissed his cheek. The caress was there and gone before his brain realized it had happened.

"Thank you for being Jack's friend."

She turned and walked away again. This time she didn't look back. Ian followed her with his eyes all the way up the street until she disappeared into the Gull. He felt lightheaded, sluggish, as if someone had slipped him a drug. Slowly he turned around and with effort propelled himself forward. He was getting in too deep, he told himself, yet he couldn't convince himself to heed the warning signs. The depths that threatened to drown him looked too inviting.

Chapter Eight

Mimi lay back on her bed, one arm over her eyes. Behind her closed lids, visions of Ian tormented her. Why had she cried all over him? And then kissed him? She had been such an *idiot*. Again. Yet, deep down, she wished she had gone for his lips instead of his cheek. With a groan, she rolled over onto her stomach and buried her face in the comforter. She wondered what he thought of her, but she was afraid she knew: she was crazy.

Sighing, she shifted to prop herself on her forearms, one fingernail picking at the quilting. He had been sweet about it, though, without a hint of arrogance. His gentle hands and strong arms felt good around her. It had been all she could do not to melt into him, to lean against his strength. Mimi glanced at the clock and pushed herself off the bed. She had no time for this useless regret and second-guessing. It had happened; it was time to forget about it.

Mimi scowled at her reflection for a moment when she stood before the mirror over the bathroom sink, then sighed. Pulling out her makeup, she applied a layer of creamy foundation to her skin. As she worked, the ritual preparation for the stage relaxed her. Thoughts of Ian receded. With a sure hand, she dramatized her eyes with liner and a smoky-gray shadow. Mascara on her lashes intensified the blue irises.

A bit of blush and a swath of rose lipstick and her face was ready for the spotlight.

The dress for tonight's performance hung over the closet door, pressed and ready. Mimi pulled it over her head and hips. Zipping up the side, she tugged gently to settle the midnight-blue chiffon into place. Fitted from bust to hips, the dress flared into tiers of ruffles that ended above her knees. Short, but not too short, the skirt was flirty and fun. The neckline veed in front and back, edged with a band of silver sequins and beads. Mimi smoothed a hand over the fabric. It shimmered as the thin silver thread in the weave caught the light. Twisting around the see the back, she straightened a ruffle that had flipped up. When she stepped into low black heels, she was ready.

"How's it going in here?" Her mother poked her head around the door. "Oh, my. You look lovely, dear."

"Thanks. Is it too fancy?" She fluffed out the top layer of ruffles.

"Oh, no. It's perfect." Claire surveyed her from head to foot. "You look like a star."

Mimi snorted. "Looks are deceiving."

"Well, you have a fan club, anyway. Patrick Berzani and his wife just arrived before I left. He said Anna's on her way as well as a few other people."

Mimi stifled a groan. "Other people" might include Ian. Friends and acquaintances she welcomed, but Ian was a unique case. Under his inscrutable gaze, she might lose some of her buoyant confidence, forget a chord, hit a wrong note, embarrass herself in a million unforeseen ways. "Well, at least I won't be singing to an empty house."

"That's not a problem, dear. It's Saturday night in the middle of the summer. The place is packed."

"Really?" A wave of anticipation surged through her, bringing a smile to her lips.

"Your public awaits," Claire said with a laugh. She hugged Mimi and patted her back. "I can't wait to hear you sing again."

"Showtime, Mom." Jack had bounded into the room. "Wow! You look pretty."

He sounded so surprised, Mimi had to laugh. "Thanks, I think."

Claire looked at the clock. "Let's get going. It's nearly nine."

As they walked downstairs and out the front door, Mimi gave Jack his orders for the evening: "You're going to have to keep a low profile tonight, kiddo. No sitting at the bar and no wandering around."

"I know, I know," Jack said, rolling his eyes as he skipped along the walkway. "I can't get Grandpop into trouble."

"And you have to be in bed by ten o'clock."

"Mo-*om*."

"No, Jacky. That's too late as it is and I'm only allowing you to stay up because it's a special occasion."

"Don't worry, dear," Claire said. "I'll make sure he gets home and into bed."

On the short path between the house and the Laughing Gull, Jack pranced and danced ahead of them, acting as excited as Mimi felt. The night air was warm and humid, slipping like silk over her skin. She could hear the sounds of revelry from the tavern. Her heart started pumping and she felt flushed. Her father was right: singing for an audience was like a drug she needed to survive.

They entered through the side door. Claire steered Jack away to the kitchen to watch from the serving station. Mimi headed for the "stage" her father had carved out on one side of the room. It wasn't much, just a stool and a table, but it would do. Her guitar case was propped in the corner, waiting for her. No microphone meant she would have to sing louder, but the venue had the right acoustics for it. Plus, her father had insisted that amplification would only destroy the beauty and purity of her voice.

As Mimi laid the case on a table, George came over with a glass of water for her. "Knock 'em dead, kid."

"Thanks, Dad." She kissed his cheek as he patted her back and moved away.

She looked at the stickers on the textured black surface of the case, each one a memory of different places, different bands, musicians, friends, fans and long hours on a bus. She savored them as if seeing them for the first time. Opening the clasps, she raised the lid and touched the guitar strings. It felt as if a heartbeat pulsed through them. She was returning, at least in a small way, to the life she had loved so much.

The guitar's polished spruce soundboard shone in the dim light. A filigree of rosewood and pearl circled the hole. Well-worn, the ebony fret board invited her fingers to play. These contours were as familiar as her own body; the sound, an extension of her own voice. The guitar had cost her the earth, but over the years seemed worth every penny, every sacrifice she had made to own it and play it.

Mimi wrapped her fingers around the neck and removed the instrument from the case. She put the strap over her shoulder. A long sigh rose out of her throat as if she had finally set down some great weight. She turned and sat on the stool, keeping her head bent, eyes closed. Her fingers found the strings and tuning keys automatically. They took their time adjusting each string. She strummed the first chords to a song she had written when she was pregnant with Jack. Through all the years it remained one of her favorites. The words rose to her lips as if they had been locked in her heart all this time. Her performance began; the long months of abstinence disappeared in a second.

The music got the attention of several patrons nearby. Her voice, starting low and husky, turned more heads as it reached the back of the room. By increments, the bar quieted so that the music rose over the scattered conversations. Mimi kept her eyes closed through the first bars of the song. As the music rose, her eyes opened and she smiled automatically at a man sitting a few feet away. His answering grin encouraged her. She winked and slid her gaze to his companion, who nodded her head in time to the music. They exchanged a friendly glance before Mimi casually caught the eye of other listeners, slowly seducing them with each note.

When the song was finished, there was applause, but she didn't stop. She sat up straighter on her stool and segued into a long ballad about life on the road. As she sang, she saw her father tending bar, her mother and Jack standing at the serving station. All sported proud smiles as wide as a sunrise. They had always been her best fans. Warmth swept across Mimi's face as she absorbed their happiness. She had finally come home.

"HEY, THE WORKDAY'S OVER. It's time to play." Anna stood in the doorway, her hands on her hips.

"This *is* play. It's for my own boat." Ian barely looked up from the piece of wood he was cutting. "So, go away."

He wasn't surprised when Anna took a few more steps into the shop. The day she listened to her brothers was the day the devil started selling Popsicles.

"You've been working on that boat for years. Aren't you finished with it yet?"

"No. It's a boat, there's always work to be done."

"So, do it tomorrow," she said, putting her hand on the wood right where Ian was setting the saw.

"Move your hand before I cut it off."

"I'm going down to the Gull. Come with me."

"No."

"Come *on,* Ian. I'm not matchmaking, I promise."

"Why don't I believe you?"

"I just want to have a last drink with my big brother. Just the two of us?"

Ian scowled. "When are you leaving, anyway?"

"Tomorrow."

With a sigh of aggravation, he propped both hands on the edge of the workbench and lowered his head. He knew he was being played. Raising his head, he looked over at her. "You remind me a lot of my mother."

She stiffened, a flush rising to her cheeks. "There's no need to get snotty about it," she said with a snap. "If you're—"

Ian grinned at her anger and felt better immediately. "Give me half an hour to take a shower. I'll meet you there."

"Great!" Anna leaned over and planted a kiss on his cheek—the second kiss on that cheek for the day. She pulled back, rubbing a hand over her lips. "Better shave, too. That's some serious bristle there."

"It's supposed to stop women from kissing me," Ian said dryly.

"I bet it doesn't," his sister replied, her dark eyes glinting with mischief. "You never know, you could meet the woman of your dreams tonight."

Ian snorted, his momentary good humor erased. "I dream about sailing my boat on the ocean where there's no women around to pester me."

Anna laughed and left the shop. Ian racked his tools and

slumped to a seat on a stool at the end of the workbench. He could feel a mistake coming. After what had happened this afternoon, the last thing he needed to see was more of Mimi Green. If he closed his eyes, he could still smell her sweet fragrance, feel her breasts pressing gently against his chest. That brief taste of her only made him want more. He rubbed his hands over his face, pressing fingertips into his eye sockets.

Please don't let me make the same mistake again.

Dropping his hands, he sighed. Somehow, he would get through the evening, have a few drinks and laughs with Anna, then get the hell out of there as quickly as possible. The good thing was that the Gull was usually busy on Saturday nights, so Mimi would be working. At worst, he would be close to her for only a few seconds.

Ian held that thought like a shield. Getting to his feet, he shut off the shop lights and locked the door behind him. Grabbing a change of clothes from the boat, he went ashore to shower in the yard facilities. As he got ready, he focused on the list of projects left to do on *Minerva,* mentally going through each item one at a time. He realized his scheme to distract himself had worked too well when he looked in the mirror: his whiskers were half gone. After an annoyed pause, he completed the job. It didn't mean anything; it was just habit. Splashing his face, he cleaned off the remaining shaving cream and stray hairs.

More than a half hour later, Ian opened the door to the Laughing Gull and stepped inside. The place was packed, but it was strangely quiet, most of the chatter a low murmur rather than the usual dull roar. Over the voices, he heard a guitar and a low, husky voice that sent a shiver over his skin. A woman was singing about love, loss and too many miles of highway. Across the room, he saw the source of the beautiful voice: Mimi Green.

Her eyes were closed as she sang, then they opened and she smiled. Ian backed up a pace or two, keeping to the shadows. She was beautiful, as always, but there was something more tonight. There was no spotlight, nothing to draw the eye to her face, but she—his mind fumbled for the word—she *glowed*. Like an inner source of light lit her face.

The door swung opened behind him, jostling his arm.

"Hey, man, you in or out?"

The voice startled Ian out of his trance. He turned his head, surprised to see Evan McKenzie. His right arm was draped over the shoulder of a buxom blonde.

"Ian! I was betting you wouldn't show up for this."

"For what?" Ian asked as he dropped a kiss on the woman's cheek. "Nice to see you, Kippy."

"You, too, Ian," the woman said with a lush red smile. Her voice was breathy, puffing on his cheek.

"Mimi's big comeback," Evan said, in answer to Ian's question. "Patrick and Anna invited everyone. They should have a table reserved for us." Evan craned his neck, scanning the crowd over Ian's shoulder. "There they are. Lead the way, man."

Evan poked Ian, pointing off to the left. Ian turned and reluctantly headed farther into the bar. When he reached the table near the windows, he saw not only Anna, but Patrick, Kate, his other sister Jeannie and her husband, Charlie. There was a flurry of cheek-kissing and hand-clasps, then Ian settled into a chair next to Anna. Evan and Kippy sat on the other side of the table, next to Kate and Patrick. Anna looked over at the new couple, frowning slightly.

Ian nudged her. "So glad that it's just the *two* of us," he hissed and pinned her with a frosty stare.

Anna shrugged innocently. Her face was solemn, but her

eyes were laughing. "Who knew there would be a party for my last night?"

Ian snorted and shook his head: his sister was impossible. Patrick poured a beer from the pitcher and slid the glass across the table to Ian. He offered the same to Evan and Kippy. She declined and asked for a strawberry daiquiri.

Anna's eyes narrowed on Evan. She leaned closer to Ian and asked, "Who's the bimbo?"

Ian took a deep drink of his beer. "His girlfriend."

"Girlfriend as in singular? Since when is Evan involved with one woman at a time?"

"Jealous?" he asked, one eyebrow raised.

Anna frowned, her dark eyes shooting sparks at him. "Why would I be—"

"Quiet, Annie," Patrick interrupted. "Some of us want to hear the music."

Anna's mouth closed with a snap and she turned her glare on Patrick. He shook his head at her, then looked over at Kate with a shrug. Jeannie tapped Patrick on the shoulder and wagged a finger at him. He stuck out his tongue, making her laugh. Evan whispered something to Kippy and she giggled. Anna glanced at them, distaste flickering over her face. Ian watched the whole interchange and sighed. *Family.*

As the table quieted, Ian let Mimi's husky voice capture his attention. From where he sat he had a clear view of her on her stool. The expressions that played across her face mesmerized him. Watching her, he found it too easy to ignore everyone around him. The crowd in the bar seemed to fade into the distance until he and Mimi were alone. He listened—awed—as she filled each word of her song with feeling, giving them life and beauty.

"She's good," he heard Patrick remark. "Did you know she could sing like this, Annie?"

"She's better than I remember," Anna said. "Hard to believe she gave it up."

"Has she made any recordings?" Kate asked.

"A few," Anna said. "I don't think any recent ones. We'll have to ask her."

Ian barely heard this conversation. Mimi's sweet voice and the chords from her guitar had seduced him much more than her kiss. He was ensnared by her siren's voice wrapping around him, drawing him deeper and deeper to a place from which he could not escape.

MIMI ENDED HER FIRST SET with a comical, pointed song about the differences between men and women. She stood for a round of applause and promised to sing more after a break. As soon as she stowed her guitar, several fans surrounded her. Some were old friends who remembered her in high school. She smiled, shook hands, autographed a few handbills and repeated the same phrase over and over: "I'm so glad you enjoyed it. Thank you."

Flushed and exhilarated, Mimi knew she hadn't played or sung this well in a very long time. Something about tonight had made the chemistry just right. A waving arm across the room caught her attention. It was Anna, beckoning her.

"Excuse me," Mimi said to the group that pressed around her makeshift stage. "I see someone that I have to talk to." Deftly, politely, she extricated herself and hurried over to embrace Anna who met her halfway.

"I am *so* impressed!" Anna said excitedly, her brown eyes sparkling with delight.

"Did you like it? I started out a little nervous, but I think pushed through it."

"Are you kidding? We've all been talking about how

good you are." Anna indicated the table behind them full of familiar faces. "Can you join us for a minute?"

"I'd love to."

Anna led Mimi to the crowded table and everyone rose to their feet. After a confusing flood of greetings, introductions and praise, Mimi found herself sandwiched between her friend and Ian. Their shoulders competed for the same space.

"Sorry," she said as her knee bumped his.

"No problem," he said, jerking away slightly.

Mimi flushed, embarrassed to be practically sitting in his lap. Ian didn't seem any happier at the situation. He surprised her when he turned and dropped his arm behind her, hooking his hand on the back of her chair. Her shoulder now brushed his chest as she was partially encompassed by his embrace. This close, she could smell his aftershave, tangy with a hint of spice. It reminded her of being in his arms all too briefly earlier.

"Better?" he asked, his dark eyes holding hers.

Mimi nodded and swallowed once. She could still feel the bristles of his beard against her lips. The roughness was gone now. Was his cheek as smooth as it looked? She wanted to lean over and find out—that and so much more.

"We want to know where we can buy some of your recordings," Anna said.

The question startled Mimi. She turned her head toward her friend and tried to smile naturally. "I don't know. I made a couple of CDs a while back, but they were distributed through a microlabel that's no longer in business."

"Well, get back in the studio, girl. We demand to hear more of you."

There was a chorus of agreement around the table. Soon everyone seemed to be talking at once, except for Ian and herself. Mimi spoke when required, but she couldn't follow any particular thread. Her attention lingered on the line of skin where she and Ian Berzani touched. His shirt and her dress covered that skin, but that did not prevent her from feeling a burning sensation. Every time he moved, her body heat rose a degree.

She didn't dare look at him again for fear of making of fool of herself. Bad enough that she could feel every breath he took. She wanted to lean into him, make his arms encircle her instead of this teasing, vague half-embrace. Would she feel his heart beating as fast as hers? When he said something to Patrick, she darted a glance at him. To her chagrin, he looked completely at ease, calm and cool.

Mimi crossed her legs to pull away from him a bit more. As she did, her skirt hem rose, baring more of her thighs. She hurriedly tugged the sparkling chiffon back to its proper place. Out of the corner of her eye, she saw Ian's head turn toward her. She felt more than saw his gaze track her movement, and looked over. Their glances met for a split second—and locked.

His dark eyes held a fire that she hadn't seen since the first day they met. Then, she had imagined that they flared with pain, or anger. This time, she saw something else: desire. Ian said nothing. Mouth dry, Mimi could not speak either. She licked her lips. Ian's arm tightened slightly, drawing her closer. He leaned in to her, and her lips parted in anticipation.

"Who's buying the next round?"

Mimi and Ian both jumped at Anna's loud question. Ian shifted, sitting up straighter. His arm relaxed and fell away from the back of her chair. Mimi looked down at her hands knotted together in her lap. The knuckles were white. She closed her eyes for a second, drawing in a deep breath. She glanced around the table, but no one seemed to have noticed anything. They were all looking at Anna.

"You asked, you buy," Evan said.

Everyone began calling orders. "Just refill the pitcher."

"I'd like another daiquiri."

"Can we switch to light beer?"

"Wait. Wait!" Anna said with a laugh. "Do I look like a waitress?"

"Yep," Evan said. "Especially if I close my eyes."

"McKenzie, if you—"

"*I'll* do it," Ian said, his tone impatient. "Better to buy a round than listen to you two bicker." He stood and snatched up the empty pitcher. After taking everyone's order, he turned to Mimi. "Give me a hand, will you?"

"Sure."

She stood, and Ian followed her through the crowded room. Halfway across, he put a hand on her back to steer her toward the right side of the bar. A waiter passed with a tray of empty glasses. Ian handed him the pitcher and kept moving. When they got near the side door, his other hand wrapped around her arm and he tugged her through the door and outside.

"This isn't the way to the bar," she said, the pounding of her heart filling her ears.

He was silent as he drew her away from the pool of light spilling over the ground and into the shadows. She stumbled a little on the uneven paving stones. Ian stopped. His hands clasped her waist, and he turned her to face him. A shiver ran over her skin: a small thrill of anticipation mingled with alarm.

"Ian?" Her voice was a whisper of sound. "What are you doing?"

Again, he kept his silence. As her sight slowly adjusted,

Mimi could only make out the shape of his head, his broad shoulders, the paler stripes on his shirt. Her hands rose and lightly—tentatively—came to a rest on his chest. He sighed as she touched him, like a breath held for an unendurable time, then released. Eyes wide, she tilted her head up, searching for an answer in his face. His head dipped toward hers and she felt his breath on her cheek, then on her lips.

Her own breath caught in her lungs, trapped by the beating of her heart. Slowly, his mouth descended to hers. First came a feather-light brush of contact, so slight it was hardly a kiss at all. Despite the softness of it, there should have been a blinding spark. Mimi felt a shock wave from her head to her toes.

The second kiss came just as carefully, but there was nothing soft about it. Ian's lips settled over hers. His arms enclosed her. Palms spread against her back, he exerted the slightest pressure, drawing her body close, then closer still. Mimi willingly fitted herself to the long, lean-muscled strength of his body. The thumping of his heart resonated in his chest like the music from her guitar. Her hands slid around Ian's neck, fingers delving into the thick curls that seemed eager to entwine them.

Ian lifted his mouth from hers for a breath of time. "Tell me why I waited so long to taste you."

She had no answer and he did not wait for one. His lips pressed to hers again. His tongue traced her lower lip, then stole into her mouth to taste her more deeply. With a soft moan, she welcomed him. She wanted more and more and *more*.

His right hand stroked up her back, following the path of her spine. Fingers meshed into the fall of her hair, he gently tugged her head back, exposing the line of her throat. Running a trail of kisses over her chin, he bit and licked as he moved his mouth downward. His other hand slid to her waist, then lower, pressing her hips to his. She felt the ridge of his erection and arched her back in instinctive need.

"Mom? Are you out here?"

The question split the silence and their secret embrace. Ian's hands lingered at her waist for a moment before he took one step away, then another. Mimi swayed for a second, dizzy and light-headed. The side door opened farther and she saw Jack stick his head out.

"Oh, there you are." He stepped out onto the patio. "Grandmom says I have to— Ian? Hi! What're you doing out here?"

"Hey, runt." Ian's voice was only slightly ragged, not so much that Jack would notice. "Your mom wanted some fresh air before she strapped on her guitar again."

Mimi was grateful that he answered Jack. Words were impossible for a few seconds. She stepped into the light flooding from the windows and laid her hand on Jack's shoulder. "What are *you* doing here, young man? It's past ten."

"Can't I stay a little longer?"

"Sorry, but it's late." Mimi stroked her hand over the side of his face.

"Please?"

"Aren't we going sailing tomorrow?" Ian asked.

"You bet!"

"Then go get some sleep. I want wide-awake crew."

Claire came through the door. "Here you are, you rascal. You're supposed to be on your way to bed. Come along now."

"See you in the morning, kiddo," Mimi said. She bent down to kiss him, but he squirmed away. "Thanks for taking him, Mom."

"Your singing was lovely. Your fans are ready for more."

Mimi turned and looked at Ian, who lingered in the dark. She couldn't read his expression. "I should get to it."

He nodded and pushed his hands into his pockets. "Yeah, Anna and Evan have probably torn each other to pieces and the rest of them are wondering where their drinks went."

"Do you need help?"

"No. I'll get them."

Mimi turned and grabbed the door handle. Ian's hand covered hers. She shivered again at his touch, swallowing hard on the desire to turn and melt into his embrace. Jack and her mother still watched, so she stepped aside and let Ian open the door. Inside, in the dim lights of the Gull, his face remained closed, but she could see a dark fire in his eyes. A shiver ran across her skin.

"Will I see you later?" she asked.

Ian was silent. He looked down, then back up into her eyes. "Yes."

A thrill ran through her, raising goose bumps across her skin. When she spoke, she was breathless. "I'll see you... after, then."

Ian nodded once and turned away. Mimi watched him disappear into the crowd, then went over to her guitar. Picking it up, she fiddled with the strings, mostly to give herself time to recover. Her brain was whirling, her tongue befuddled. The minutes they had spent in the dark still pulsed through her. Somehow, she had to channel her desire into her music. Her fingers began strumming a love song a friend of hers had written long ago. The chords flowed through her hands and into the guitar, wrapping the crowd in warmth. *Yes,* her heart sang. Yes to anything at all.

Chapter Nine

Ian leaned against the end of the bar waiting for his drinks. George had two assistants helping him tonight. All three worked at full speed, trying to keep up with the orders. He tapped a fold of bills on the counter, feeling caged, impatient. A couple walked through the front entrance and right past where he stood. *Leave,* common sense advised him. *Get out while you still can.* Ian glanced at the door, considering this safest of options, but didn't move.

Behind him, he heard Mimi's voice rise in song once again. He closed his eyes and let it transport him back to the warm shadows outside the Gull. Her body was imprinted on his, her taste on his tongue. That flavor had him thirsting for more. Ian forced his eyes open and shook his head to clear it. What was he doing?

Patrick appeared at his side. "What's taking so long?"

"They're slammed."

His brother watched the bartenders for a moment, then turned to Ian. "I saw you and Mimi take a detour."

The words caught Ian off guard. "She wanted some fresh air."

"Right. And Evan's a candidate for the priesthood."

"It was nothing."

Patrick laughed. "Come on, bro. I may be married, but I'm not dead. I know lust when I see it."

Ian swore softly and ran a hand over his head. He thought about denying the accusation again, but knew it was pointless. "Did anyone else notice?"

"I know Anna caught it. You owe her for running interference for you. If Evan had sniffed anything unusual, he would have roasted you alive. Luckily, he was busy keeping Kippy's hands where they belong." Patrick shook his head. "He sure can pick 'em."

"Or they pick him," Ian suggested. Neither of them had ever been able to solve the puzzle of Evan's love life in all the years they had known him.

"So, what about you? Did you pick Mimi or did she pick you?"

"Neither." Ian looked away from his brother. Part of him wanted to tell Patrick to get lost, but part of him wanted—needed—to talk about the mess he had fallen into. He brought his gaze back to Patrick's. "I leave in three months. I can't get serious about her."

"You telling that to me or yourself?"

"Myself, I guess," Ian admitted. He sighed, a sharp burst of air from his lungs. "I've been down this road before, Patty."

"What makes you so sure it's the same one? Mimi isn't Caroline."

"No, she's not, but she's tied to the land. She's got Jack and he needs a stable home right now. She can't just jump aboard *Minerva* and go gallivanting around the world with me, even if she wanted to."

Patrick's eyebrows rose. "Wow. This has gone a lot further than I suspected."

"No, it hasn't." Ian's jaw clenched. "And it's not going to."

"But—"

"Let's say I get involved with Mimi." Ian's eyes met

Patrick's. "Am I supposed to give up everything I've planned for the past eight years? Again? How many times do I put my dreams on hold for other people?"

"I know, I know. First Caroline, then Dad's cancer." Now it was Patrick who sighed. "If you don't go now, you might not get another chance."

"Bingo."

"So, what are you going to do?" Patrick asked.

"Stay as far away from her as I can and keep my hands to myself," Ian said dryly.

"That sounds like a plan." Patrick grinned. "One doomed to fail, but at least it's a plan."

Ian had to laugh at that.

George set down a pitcher in front of him and the other drinks in quick succession. Ian paid, picked up the pitcher, then the two glasses of white wine for Kate and Anna. Patrick grabbed Kippy's daiquiri and the red wine for Jeannie. They threaded their way back through the tables, Patrick leading the way.

Once the drinks were distributed, Ian sat and looked over at Mimi. She still glowed, still captured her audience with her song. He sipped his beer and let her voice seep into him. But only so far. Talking to Patrick had cleared his head. His dream—his *chance*—meant more to him than this attraction to Mimi. He could not let himself be waylaid again. As her music swirled around him and pulled him in, Ian sucked in a deep breath. His path was clear. Now he just had to keep from straying off it.

MIMI PACKED UP her guitar and stowed it behind the bar. As soon as he had a moment, her father came over and hugged her.

"Great job, Mim."

"Thanks, Dad," Mimi said. "I owe it all to my pushy publicity agent."

"See," George said, giving her a little shake. "You should listen to your old man more often."

Mimi laughed and rolled her eyes. "Okay, but I'm only going to say it once—you were right."

"Can I get that in writing?" George asked with a laugh.

"Not on your life!"

"How about a glass of wine? I'll open the best bottle in the cellar, just for you."

"That would be great." Mimi scanned the gathering. "I want to talk to Anna. She's leaving tomorrow."

"I'm not sure she's still here," George said as he opened a bottle and poured. "I haven't seen her since Patrick, Kate and Ian left."

Mimi faltered as she took the glass he offered, spilling a little on her hand. "Ian left?"

"A few minutes ago. Excuse me." George took an order for two gin and tonics. He made a shooing gesture with his hands and Mimi edged into the crowd, hoping her father was mistaken.

After a fruitless circuit of the room, she slipped out through the side door into the darkness. Ian was not there, either. She took a swallow of her wine, but it was tasteless. With a shaking hand, she set the glass down on the windowsill. Wrapping her arms around herself, Mimi stood motionless. She could not go back inside and pretend to smile. Home called to her, a comforting haven where she could be alone.

Alone.

Walking slowly down the path, she stopped halfway. Closing her eyes, she tilted her head back. The stars twinkled down at her, made even more brilliant by the glaze of tears in her eyes. The exhilaration of the evening was gone, lost in the bewilderment of Ian's sudden departure. Sighing, she straightened and moved forward. A large shape loomed out of the darkness and she couldn't control her squeak of fright.

"Mimi?"

"Ian! You scared the bejesus out of me," she said, one hand at her throat. "What are you doing out here?"

He stepped forward, his shirt a pale blur in the night. "Sorry. It got too crowded inside."

Mimi swallowed. "Dad said you left."

He seemed to weigh the statement carefully. With the streetlight behind him, she couldn't read his face. "I did," he said finally. "I didn't plan to come back."

"Then why did you?"

"Because I would be a coward if I hadn't."

Ian said this so quietly she wasn't sure she heard him correctly. A shiver ran over her skin that had nothing to do with the cool night air.

"Look, can we go somewhere and talk?" he asked.

Mimi opened her mouth and came close to saying no. But she wanted to know why he had left. "Okay. Where do you want to go?"

"My boat."

Ian led the way to the street. There, he turned toward the marina. They walked in silence, not touching, his pace matched to hers across the gravel parking lot. As they went down the ramp onto the docks, he pointed to the gaps in the planks.

"Be careful. Your heels might get caught."

Mimi stopped and slipped off her shoes and picked them up. As she did, Ian took her hand to steady her, his warm, callused grip enveloping hers. When she straightened, he didn't let go, and Mimi let her hand rest in his. There was a feeling of comfort and safety in his touch, as well as the sweet slide of anticipation. Padding along barefoot at his side, she didn't speak again until he stopped alongside a sailboat. *Minerva* was carved into a curved board on the transom.

"Watch your step."

He stepped aboard first and held out his hand to help her. She followed him to the cockpit. Pushing open a hatch, he lifted out two boards, then climbed down into the cabin. Once inside, he flipped a switch, illuminating the passage for her. In the wash of light, Mimi saw a tiny galley with a sink and stove. She could see louvered doors above the cream-colored countertops. The varnished woodwork gleamed.

"She's beautiful."

"Come on down," Ian said softly.

Mimi left her shoes in the cockpit and backed down the ladderlike steps. Turning around at the bottom, she surveyed the cabin interior. Across from the galley was a navigation table and forward was the saloon. Long, built-in settees stretched along each side of the cabin, the upholstery deep green with a small pattern in a lighter color.

Ian switched on more lights. The small puddles of illumination enlarged the intimacy and revealed more details. Behind the settees were more louvered doors and a couple of open shelves filled with books. Between the settees was a drop-leaf table, teak with an inlay of a lighter wood in the shape of a compass rose. Over it was a hatch surrounded in more teak. The rest of the ceiling was white. Forward of the saloon, Mimi could see another passageway into what must be the sleeping quarters and the head.

He motioned her to a seat. "Do you want something to drink?"

"No, thank you." She doubted she would be able to

swallow anything. "This is a lovely boat. I don't have to ask who built it. All these details in the woodwork, these cabinets, the table. It must have taken you a while."

"Four years." His eyes locked on hers. The desire she had seen earlier shone clearly once more. Mimi took one step, then another, until she was mere inches away from Ian. Slowly, his hand rose, his fingers just brushing her cheek.

"This is not supposed to happen," he said in a whisper.

"Don't say that." This time, she didn't hesitate. Her arms encircled his neck and she pressed against him lightly.

As before, his arms closed around her, intensifying that pressure. With a groan, his head dipped to hers and their mouths met. This time, there was nothing tentative about his kiss. His lips covered hers and his tongue demanded entry to her mouth. Mimi willingly gave in, anxious for the flavor that was Ian Berzani.

Their tongues stroked, tangled, then slid free only to touch once again. Mimi moaned when his mouth left hers, then shivered as his teeth found the tender lobe of her ear. She felt as if she was floating. She was. Ian had picked her up and lowered her to the cushioned settee. He came down beside her, one leg across hers. He stroked one hand down her arm, then back up, threading his fingers into her hair to hold her still for his kiss.

Soon that hand found its way to her breast, cupping the soft mound, shaping it gently. When his thumb stroked over her nipple, an electric thrill shot straight to her toes.

"Do that again," she said, her voice a whisper against his lips. She wound her leg around his, smoothing her foot over his calf.

Ian's head rose. He gazed down at her, dark eyes unfocused. His thumb stroked across her once more and Mimi sighed, arching into the touch. She lifted a hand to his face, urging him down. She wanted his lips against hers again, his body and more. Ian's head descended an inch, then stopped.

"No. This is wrong." He closed his eyes tightly, then opened them to look at her once again. His gaze was sharper now, cleansed of passion. In one lithe movement, Ian was off the settee. She lay where she was, confused, chilled. He stood with his back to her, hands braced on the companionway steps, as if he was getting ready to flee. He dropped his head down and he took several deep breaths. Mimi watched him for a moment, then sat up. Her skirt had ridden up on her thighs. She tugged the fabric down and plucked at the ruffles, straightening the crumpled fabric.

"I'm sorry," Ian said, his voice low, rusty. He turned around and looked at her. His jaw was set, his eyes opaque. "This was a mistake."

Mimi glanced up at him, then lowered her eyes. "I—" Bewildered, she fumbled for what she should say. Nobody had ever apologized for kissing her. "Why?"

"It's wrong. For both of us."

"But why?" she asked again, staring at him with dawning comprehension. "Oh, no. You're *married!*"

"No!" Ian shook his head. "No. I'm not married or even involved with anyone." He sighed and leaned back against the steps. "That's the point."

"I don't understand."

Sighing again, he came and sat next to her on the settee. "I know. That's why I wanted to talk to you tonight. Because you *don't* understand."

"So, tell me."

"In three months, I'm leaving." Ian linked his hands together and rested his forearms on his knees. He did not look at her. "I'm going to sail this boat around the world. I'll be gone for several years."

"Oh." Mimi's tumult and fears began to settle. "So, that's why... Oh, I see."

Ian straightened. "I've been planning this for a long time, Mimi. Eight *years*. Every time I get close to slipping the lines, something happens to stop me. My dad had cancer, the yard needed me, a—" He stopped. "I *can't* get involved with you, then just end it and leave."

His eyes locked on hers and, for just a moment, Mimi saw the whirling emotions in their dark depths. To glimpse such passion, distress and tenderness in such a strong man set her heart pounding. She *yearned* for him to take her in his arms. But he would not let her.

"It hurts," she said. Her voice almost broke with repressed anguish. *No.* She would *not* cry, not here, not now. "But I understand."

"Do you?" His eyes searched hers.

Twisting her hands together in her lap, Mimi nodded. "Probably better than most." Bravely, she smiled at him. "I chased a dream for ten years myself. I know what it is to have something just out of your reach. Just *there*." One hand went out to grab something invisible, drifting through the air. "Yet, no matter how much you sacrifice and work, you can't quite touch it."

They were silent together for a while, lost in their own thoughts. Finally, he looked over at her again. His eyes were sad now. "You make me want to stay."

Mimi nearly cried out in pain. "Thank you. I'm flattered," she said softly. And she was.

"How is that flattery?"

"That I can tempt you away from your dream?" Mimi reached out and brushed her fingers over his cheek. "Oh, yes. That's definitely something special."

He caught her hand and kissed it. "We could have an affair. For three months."

She laughed, knowing that a little wouldn't satisfy either of them and might even trap him. "Don't tempt *me*."

Ian looked down at the floor, still holding her hand. "You could always come with me." His voice was low, his face averted.

Mimi closed her eyes, considering this fantasy. In another place and time, she might have accepted the offer. She could imagine the two of them alone on the ocean or exploring far-off places. She squeezed his hand. "No. This is your time to dream. It's my time to be responsible. For Jack."

"I understand. Bad timing for both of us." Ian kissed the back of her hand once more, then rose, bringing her to her feet with him. "I'd better take you home."

Mimi let herself be led out of the cabin and back down the dock. Once ashore, she slipped into her shoes and walked beside Ian to her parents' home. There, under the amber glow of the porch light, she kissed him on the cheek.

"Good night. I'll miss you. I'll miss what we might have had."

"I am sorry, Mimi," Ian said, his hands cupping her shoulders.

"Me, too." She didn't bother to try to smile this time. She couldn't, not when her heart was breaking.

With that, she went inside, shutting the door behind her and leaning against the panels. She heard him leave, his footsteps fading into the night, and a tear tracked down her cheek. Mimi turned out the lights and slowly climbed the stairs. She would cry tonight for what might have been, then tomorrow she would get on with her life, a life without Ian Berzani.

Chapter Ten

By the next morning, Mimi had decided the best plan was to avoid Ian. If she couldn't have him, she didn't think she could bear being near him. And even if they pretended to be friends, the truth of their almost love would be there, looming. And she wouldn't—couldn't—risk temptation, potentially sabotaging his plans. He deserved the chance to seize his dream. In time, Mimi told herself, Ian would be just a memory and she would move on with her life. It was a good, practical solution, except for the one unpredictable element she loved but couldn't control.

Jack.

To her surprise and delight, her son plugged away at summer school with a minimum of protest and whining. Of course, by doing so, he earned the reward of Sunday afternoons on *Minerva*. He also saw Ian on Saturday mornings at his sailing class. When Jack came home, every third word was *Ian,* followed by *said, did* or *had.* All this talk about the man she was supposed to forget stung Mimi's heart.

Weekday afternoons, whenever Mimi would let him—and sometimes when she had *not*—Jack went over to A&E Marine. More than once she had to track him down and drag him home. That meant she had to talk to Ian. These encounters were awkward for both of them. She apologized for Jack's intrusion, but Ian only shrugged and told her that he enjoyed having her son around.

After their second Sunday sail, Mimi came to the boat to round up her son. On the walk home, she asked Jack if he knew about Ian's plan to sail *Minerva* around the world.

"Yeah! Isn't that the coolest? Can I go with him?"

Mimi laughed. "Certainly not. You have to stay here and finish school."

Jack spied a large chunk of gravel and kicked it as hard as he could. "I figured you'd say that."

As the summer progressed, so did the bond between Ian and Jack. Mimi could wish her son would worship someone else. Jack had never lacked male role models. Other men—musicians, sound techs, bartenders, friends—had taken an interest in him over the years. He had returned the favor with his young awe and admiration. But Jack had never latched on to one man as he had to Ian Berzani.

Watching them together, Mimi realized that Jack had been waiting for Ian, or somebody like him: a patient and kind man, one who could be his hero, his friend, his guide. When he needed a confidant, Ian was there. If he needed a buddy, Ian was one. If he needed encouragement, Ian gave it. When Jack was out of line, Ian corrected him. Jack responded to these reprimands with sulks and stomps, but in the end changed his behavior for the better. Jack loved Ian.

The problem was, Mimi did, too. But there was nothing she could do about it, nothing she *would* do. She just had to hang on, dying a little inside every time she saw him, or heard Jack's praise. Time would solve her problem, she just had to get through the next few months.

Coming home one Thursday after class, Jack sang along to the radio, between telling Mimi about his day. Mimi pulled the car into the driveway and turned off the engine.

Opening her door, she was hit with all the heat and humidity the first of August could throw at her. This was usually the hottest month for Crab Creek.

Jack popped out of the car and came around to her side. "Can I go down to the yard?"

"Not today. After lunch, Grandmom is going to take you to get new shoes."

Jack groaned dramatically. "But I—"

"Don't give me a hard time, bucko," Mimi said, putting her hand on his head and tilting his face to hers. "You can see Ian another time."

"You're no fun," Jack said with a pout. He twisted away from her, dashing for the front door. "What's for lunch?"

"Eel pie with worms."

"Gross!" Jack laughed and rolled his eyes. "I want peanut butter."

"With or without?"

"What kind of jam is there?"

"Strawberry or grape."

"With. Strawberry." He dropped his backpack on the floor inside the door.

"Hey! Take that upstairs."

"Aw, can't I eat first?"

"Go. And wash your hands while you're there," Mimi said as Jack picked up the bag and dragged it up the stairs, letting it thump against every step. She laughed and shook her head. "I foresee a great future for you on the stage."

Shooting her a glowering look that wouldn't hold, Jack bounded up the rest of the stairs and disappeared. Mimi set her purse on the hall table and went into the kitchen to make lunch. Claire was already there, mixing dough in a large ceramic bowl. A bag of apples was on the counter to one side.

"Hi, Mom. Oh, are you making a pie?"

"Yes. Your father had a craving, so I thought I'd indulge him. How did Jack do in school today?"

"He claims it went well. And he actually forgot to tell me how stupid the whole thing was."

Claire chuckled. "He's falling down on the job, then."

"He enjoys it," Mimi whispered. "But don't tell him I said that."

Mimi opened the cupboard and pulled out a jar of chunky peanut butter. She took down a plate and got a knife out of the drawer, then went to the refrigerator for jam. "Do you want a sandwich? Today's special is peanut butter."

"Does he ever eat anything else?"

Mimi laughed. "Never. My son is a creature of habit."

"I think I'll pass just this once."

Mimi smeared peanut butter on a slice of bread, then added a generous dollop of jam before putting another piece on top. She cut the sandwich in half. "May I have one of those apples for him?"

"Of course." Claire neatly quartered and cored an apple.

Mimi was pouring a tall glass of milk just as Jack raced into the kitchen.

"Mom! Guess what?"

"Lunch is ready?"

"No! I just heard—"

"Sit first, then tell me your news." She put a hand on his shoulder and nudged him to the table.

"Mo-*om*. This is important," Jack said with a scowl.

"So is lunch." Hearing his huff of impatience, she put her hands on her hips. "All right already. What?"

"Johnny Sinclair is playing at the Monument club!"

Claire shot her daughter a swift glance, forming the piecrust dough into a ball. Mimi froze for a split second, then dropped her hands to her sides. "How nice for Mr. Sinclair."

"The concert's next week. Can we go hear him? Please?"

"You're nine, Jack."

"But he's the best."

"The Monument is a nightclub. No kids allowed." She smiled, trying to soften the news. "Not every bar owner is as lenient as your grandpop."

Jack sagged into his chair and picked up half his sandwich. "It's not fair," he said around a mouthful of peanut butter and jelly.

"You'll be grown up soon enough and you can see all the concerts you want," Claire said with calm assertion.

Jack grunted unhappily and kept eating. Mimi put away the peanut butter, jam and milk, before opening the dishwasher and dropping the knife into the cutlery basket. She focused completely on each small task, letting them calm her.

"What time do we have to go, Grandmom?"

"As soon as you're done eating." Claire put the dough in the refrigerator to chill.

Jack began chugging his milk as if it was the last glass he would ever get.

"Slow down or you'll drown," Mimi scolded.

"Can I go down to the yard after me and Grandmom get back?" Jack asked, biting into a slice of apple.

"*Grandmom and I.* Not today."

"But I gotta work on the boat that me and Ian are building," Jack wailed.

"Tomorrow." Mimi held firm. "You spent all yesterday afternoon with him. Give the man a break once in a while. He does have work to do, you know."

Jack frowned. "He never cares if I hang around."

"*I* care." Mimi turned to her mother. "I'm going upstairs to change. Thanks for taking Jack to do this."

"We won't be too long. Unless we happen to stop for ice cream."

"Yeah!" Jack bounced out of his chair. "I want a scoop of strawberry and one of peanutty delight."

"First, put your dishes in the dishwasher," Claire said.

Mimi left the kitchen, went up to her room and closed the door behind her. There, she sat on the bed for a minute, then fell backward to lie staring up at the ceiling. *Johnny Sinclair.* Just thinking the name put a bitter taste on her tongue. Hearing it from her son—*their* son—was worse. Mimi closed her eyes and sighed. Now he would be here, invading her town. What did it signify? Probably nothing. After all these years, Johnny had yet to make an appearance in Jack's life. She doubted he would suddenly decide to do so now.

Pushing herself up from the bed, she changed into a pair of tailored shorts and a dark green T-shirt with the Laughing Gull logo across the back. At the same time, she pushed Johnny Sinclair into the nether reaches of her mind where he belonged. She wished he would vanish completely, but Johnny still lurked in the shadows, ready to jump out and startle her. He was the father of her child. Time did not change that. It never would.

IAN WORKED THROUGH THE afternoon with one eye on the door to the shop, expecting Jack to burst through it at any moment. When three o'clock came and went, he had to assume that Jack was not going to put in an appearance today, which disappointed him. Even though the kid constantly asked questions and got into everything, Ian enjoyed his company. Jack needed a firm hand on his tiller, but he was smart, inquisitive and entertaining. Ian genuinely liked the boy.

Two weeks ago, they had started a project together, building an Optimist pram for Jack. Constructing any boat—even this pint-size one—took work, but it was not too complicated for a dedicated nine-year-old who had supervision. First, they had laid the paper patterns out and carefully marked the plywood pieces. After they cut these, Jack drilled small holes in the edges. Then assembly began. They strung short lengths of copper wire through the holes and twisted them tight, cinching the pieces together. Then they covered the seams in thick epoxy to strengthen them. Now the pram, upside down on two sawhorses in the corner of the shop, waited for more coats of epoxy and a few coats of paint.

Building the pram kept Jack busy. And, Ian had to admit to himself, kept the kid at the shop for long hours. That meant that Mimi often came to fetch him. These brief encounters were Ian's secret vice. Mimi remained the one thing he knew he shouldn't have, but couldn't keep from wanting. He told himself that as long as he didn't touch her, as long as their conversation was about Jack, the Gull, his work, her singing, he was safe. They just had to make it through the next couple of months without doing something stupid. And yet, it was as though the more they avoided talking about how they felt, the bigger and more dangerous those feelings got.

The door to the shop creaked open, startling Ian from his thoughts. Jack rushed in and let the door slam behind him.

"Hey, runt. I wondered where you were."

"I had to go get new shoes."

Ian looked at the tattered, dirt-stained tennis shoes Jack wore. "They selling preworn ones now?"

Jack giggled. "No. These are my old ones. Mom'd kill me if I got gunk on the new ones right away."

"Smart man," Ian said with a nod.

"Can we work on my boat today?"

"Sure, we've got time to lay up another layer on the keel."

"Yeah!" Jack bounced over to the shelves where Ian kept all the epoxy and adhesives. He snapped on a pair of latex gloves and looked over at Ian. "Should I mix up the same stuff we used yesterday?"

Ian pulled a roll of fiberglass mesh out of a bin. The strands were woven into a thin cloth. "Cut a strip of this first."

Jack got the scissors. "How wide?"

"I'd say about three inches for the first pass. How much for the strip on top of that?"

"Two inches wider than the one below it, right?"

"Exactly." Ian handed Jack a tape measure. "Check how long the piece should be before you get gooped up with epoxy."

Jack measured and cut. Ian kept an eye on him as he finished a set of three drawer fronts. As they both worked, Jack chattered about school and a story he had read about a girl who grew up in Africa. Ian shook his head as he listened. Where was the kid who said he hated school?

When Jack finished cutting, Ian helped him mix up a batch of epoxy. "Make sure the fabric is completely saturated," Ian said.

"It's clear all the way through." Jack's face was intent, his brow furrowed in concentration. He dabbed at the fiberglass cloth in place on the keel. "How do I get the bubbles out again?"

"Use that roller. Work from the center out."

"Oops, I got a drip." Jack grabbed a paper towel and smeared away the excess epoxy without being told.

Ian patted him on the back. "You know what you're doing." He went back to his workbench and let Jack apply the second layer by himself.

"I think I'm done," Jack said. "Come look."

Ian set down his sanding block and moved over to the small boat. The fiberglass lay in a glistening line down the outside of the keel. It looked smooth and even. "Perfect. How many layers total?"

"Four. Two yesterday and two today. Is that strong enough?"

"Should be. We'll test it tomorrow and see." Ian laid a hand on Jack's shoulder.

Jack grinned up at him, peeled off his gloves and threw them in the trash. The door opened and a slant of sunlight washed across the floor as a tall man with dark hair going silver stepped inside.

"Hey, Pop," Ian said.

"The bronze screws you ordered for *Thalia* came in." Ian's father dropped a small box on the workbench.

"Jack, this is my father, Antonio Berzani. Pop, this is Jack Green, George's grandson."

Antonio solemnly shook the boy's hand. "I am very pleased to meet you."

Jack ducked his head shyly. "Nice to meet you," he said in a mumble.

"We were just looking over Jack's work," Ian said. "He's building an Optimist."

Carefully, taking time to check the seams, epoxy and fiberglass, Antonio surveyed Jack's work. "You did this?" he asked, looking intently at the boy.

"Ian showed me what to do, but I laid this up all on my

own," Jack said proudly. His shyness evaporated under the calm attention of the older man.

"This is very good work." Antonio looked over at Ian. "Have you offered him a job yet? We can't let such a good worker get away from us."

Jack giggled.

"Not yet. I will as soon I see how he finishes this."

"I am going over to Freeman's to pick up an order. Do you need anything?"

"Nope. I'm set."

Antonio nodded, then looked down at Jack. "Keep up the good work. This will be a fine sailboat when you are finished."

Jack tried to hide behind his bangs, but Ian saw the pleased embarrassment on his face. Antonio smiled, patted Ian on the shoulder and left them. Next, Ian showed Jack how to sand the pieces of plywood that would form the rudder and daggerboard, then went back to work on his own project. Jack was silent as he sanded, which was unusual.

"Your dad's nice," he said finally.

"I think so, too."

"I don't have a dad."

Ian looked over at Jack, but the boy kept his face averted. He set down his block of sandpaper. What the hell was he supposed to say to that?

"You've got a great mom."

"Yeah. I guess."

Before Ian could comment further, the door to the shop swung open again and Mimi walked inside.

"Hello, Ian." She flicked him a glance, but her eyes were centered on Jack. "I thought I told you that you couldn't come here today," she said sternly.

"But that was before."

"Jack, I told you not today," Mimi said. "That means *all* day."

"But I just came over for a little while."

"Didn't you tell me you have homework?"

"Only one page of math. That's hardly *any*thing!"

Ian listened to the battle rage without really hearing it. Seeing Mimi so suddenly seemed to have jarred something loose inside. Her face was angry, brows drawn together as she argued with Jack. She had a smear of something damp on her shirt and her ponytail was lopsided. Still, she was prettier than any woman he had ever seen. He wanted her more than he had ever wanted another soul on earth. The truth struck Ian like a hammer blow.

I love her.

He shook his head, but Mimi and Jack paid no heed and kept arguing. It couldn't be true, Ian thought. They had known each other for such a short time. He had plans. She had commitments. There were a hundred reasons why it could *not* be true.

"But, Jack, what did I say?"

"Not to come down here today." Jack squirmed and hung his head.

"Finally, we agree. We're going home. Now. We'll discuss this on the way back."

With a sigh, Jack set down his sandpaper. He walked over to his mother, scuffing his feet on the concrete as he went. Mimi put one hand on his shoulder and steered him toward the door.

"Bye, Ian," she said, her face still full of ire. "Jack will see you another day."

The door closed behind them and Ian stared at it. "I can't be in love with her," he said aloud in the ringing silence of the room.

His denial had no effect. His heart knew the truth, even

if his head was running in panic. Slumping to a seat on a stool, Ian propped his elbows on the workbench and dropped his head into his hands. He had tried so hard avoid this trap, but here he was again. What was he supposed to do now? He looked around and saw no escape.

Chapter Eleven

Mimi set her tray on the table and gathered up the empty glasses and beer bottles. With a flick of a damp cloth, she wiped the table clean, then hoisted the tray. Balancing her load with one hand, she wove her way back through the bar, stopping at tables as she passed. A couple at the window ordered more beer. A foursome at table seven wanted chips and salsa as well as another round of margaritas. Table three was ready for their check, so she cashed them out and sent them off with a smile.

George came out of the kitchen, wiping his hands on a bar towel. He'd been in the stockroom, shifting boxes around. "How did we end up with two cases of raspberry vodka?"

"Don't look at me," Mimi said as she swished glasses through the wash and into the rinse water.

"Must be left over from the New Year's Eve bash."

"I see raspberry martinis will be this month's special."

George laughed as he poured a beer for a customer down the bar. Mimi collected money and dirty glasses from a couple who were finished for the evening. Dumping the glasses in the sink, she made change and waved the two regulars goodbye.

"Can you take over for a few?" she asked George.

"No problem. Going to check on Jack?"

"You got it. He's overdrawn his trustworthiness account." Mimi pursed her lips. "I've got to make sure he's doing what he promised to do."

"He just likes to be around Ian, Mim," George said with a chuckle. "I'd want to be down at the marina, working on a boat myself."

"But when I say no, he has to obey me. Is that too strict?"

"No. You balance well—you give him boundaries where he needs them, but you're careful not to stifle him."

Mimi felt a rush of satisfaction from her father's praise. "Plus, Ian needs a break. The man has a job. Jack can't go over there every afternoon and get in the way."

"Does Ian complain?"

"No, but—"

"Ian's a big boy. If he didn't want Jack around, he'd figure out a way to get rid of him."

"Maybe so. I just don't want to take advantage of him." Mimi chewed the inside of her lip. "Anyway, I'll be back in a few minutes."

Mimi walked over to the house and opened the door quietly. She sneaked up the stairs as silently as she could. The door to Jack's room was ajar just enough so she could peek in without being seen. Lo and behold, there he sat at his desk, pencil in hand, engrossed in his math workbook. Mimi resisted the urge to barge in and give him a kiss on his blessed little cheek. Instead, she went back outside and raised both fists in the air and did a victory dance on the front porch. Then she went back to work.

"Thanks," she told her father. "You can get out of here for a while if you want."

George glanced over her shoulder, then looked back at her. "Mim, there's someone here to see you."

"Who?" For some reason, she hoped it might be Ian.

He looked past her again and Mimi turned, following his gaze. Before she could speak, she was snared by brilliant blue eyes that exactly matched a photo she had once seen of the Aegean Sea. The man's blond hair was short and stylishly spiked up in the front. A half-dozen earrings decorated one ear and a tattoo wrapped around his wrist. Mimi's mouth dropped open with dread. It could *not* be. It must not be.

When he smiled at her, she knew it *was*. A mischievous, charming grin with its flaw of slightly overlapping front teeth confirmed it. Her head felt light. Her gut tightened. Then he got off the stool and came toward her. He still wore the same attire, as if he had never worn anything else: a concert T-shirt, blue jeans torn and faded in all the right spots and black boots. He put his arms around her and hugged her tightly.

"Hey, Mimi," Johnny Sinclair said. "Did you miss me?"

Her arms hung stiffly at her sides. She reminded herself that for better or worse, this was Jack's father. Mimi closed her eyes and breathed in his scent, still familiar after all these years. It reminded her of the fights, the long, lonely nights, the days of uncertainty.

She drew back and met his eyes. "I'm impressed. You remembered my name."

Johnny kept his hands on her shoulders and laughed. "Haven't changed much, have you? Still the same direct, no-nonsense Mimsy." His eyes gleamed as he gave her a thorough once-over. "Still beautiful, too."

She pulled away from his touch. The bar had gone silent when Johnny stood up and hugged her. Or maybe it had been quiet before and she hadn't noticed. Now it seemed that everyone in the place was watching her and Johnny.

She didn't need an audience for what she wanted to say to him. Grabbing his arm, she led him to the back door. Her father could manage without her for a bit longer.

Mimi pushed through the door and Johnny followed her outside. This side of the building was in shadow, the sun down behind the trees, but it was still hot and muggy. Two more steps and she turned to face her former lover.

"You know the first year, I hoped you'd come back. Then for a while, I decided I didn't care if you did or not," she said, folding her arms across her chest. "Now, I wish you hadn't."

"I missed you, too. It seems like yesterday, doesn't it?" Johnny still had that cocky grin that used to make her heart swoon.

"No. It seems like nine years, ten months and fourteen days."

"You're keeping a count. That's sweet."

"That's how old Jack is." Mimi reined in her temper. "What are you doing here?"

"I was in town, so I thought I'd stop by," he said with a shrug. "I heard you were back."

"Why don't I believe that?" Mimi narrowed her eyes.

He stuck his hands in his pockets and turned his head, scrutinizing the small patio. He took a few steps away from her. "I don't know. I guess it seemed like the right time," he said finally. Turning back, he met her gaze. "Sorry it's been so long."

Nodding, Mimi looked down at the ground, then back into Johnny's clear blue eyes. "You can't see him."

"He's my kid, too, y'know."

"No, he isn't," Mimi said fiercely. She was suddenly, incandescently angry. Protective instincts rose in her like a tidal wave. She leaned forward, nearly hissing her words. "He's *mine*. I raised him. I helped him take his first steps and sat up worried all night when he was sick. I taught him to read and to ride a bike, picked him up when he fell, bandaged his scrapes and made sure he was happy. I did *everything*. You did nothing. So, don't think you can waltz in here and pretend to be his father."

"Whoa, whoa, *whoa!*" Johnny raised his hands up in defense. "Did I say that's what I was going to do?" When Mimi didn't answer, he shook his head at her. "Jeez, calm down, Mimsy. I want to see the kid. That's all."

Mimi eyed him warily. "I'll make a video and post it on the Internet."

"Who are you protecting?"

Mimi stared at Johnny, unable to believe he was so obtuse. "Look. You're his father. The man he's been missing his entire life." She shook her head in disgust. "If that's not bad enough, you're also a famous rock star. One he idolizes, in fact. He's not going to understand why you—one of his heroes and his *father*—abandoned him. It's going to hurt and I don't want that to happen."

"It wasn't like I planned to get famous and—"

"*Bullshit,* Johnny," Mimi said harshly. "Fame is all you've ever cared about. That's why you walked away from me and Jack. We got in your way."

Johnny stiffened and his hands balled into fists. "Come on, that's not true!"

"Yes, it *is*." Mimi speared him with a direct look, daring him to refute her. "If you want to see him, don't start by lying."

He glared back at her, his blue eyes boiling with enough temper to match hers. Then he gave a short, sharp laugh. Rubbing a hand over his face, Johnny paced away from her. He stood with his back to her for a long minute, then turned around. "Has he asked about me?" he asked softly.

"He's asked if he *had* a father. But he never mentioned

you, specifically." Seeing his downcast face, Mimi sighed. Her fury had drained away, leaving her sad and tired. It was pointless being angry at Johnny. Too many years had passed. "Look, he hasn't missed having a father in a long time. He sees that other kids don't have one at home, either. I think he just accepts that that's the way it is for him."

Johnny came back to her and put his hands on her shoulders. "I want to meet him, Mimi. With your permission. Please."

"I don't know, Johnny." She bit her lip, debating.

"I just want to get to know him a little," Johnny said. A slight smile lifted one corner of his mouth. "We don't even have to deal with the whole father thing right now. All he needs to know is that I'm an old friend of yours."

Suspicious, Mimi kept her eyes locked on his. He seemed sincere, but he had always managed to look that way. "What would you say to him?"

"You said he likes my music, right? You're just introducing him to a guy he admires." He squeezed her shoulders. "When he's ready, we—I mean, *you*—can decide what to tell him about us."

Mimi took a deep breath. "I'll think about it, Johnny."

"Can't you see that—"

"No." She held up a hand to stop him. "I won't rush this. Not when Jack's heart is at stake."

Johnny opened his mouth to protest, then closed it. Stepping back, he nodded to her. "Okay. Take a few days and think it over. I'm around for a while." He reached into his back pocket and took out his wallet. Handing her a white card, he said, "I wrote down my phone numbers for you. Call me anytime."

Mimi watched him as he walked away. A shiver tracked across her skin despite the heat. She wrapped her arms around herself.

Before he reached the street, Johnny stopped and pivoted to face her. "I've changed, Mimi. Give me a chance to prove it. And give Jack a chance to meet his father."

With that, he was gone. Mimi stared after him, tears welling up in her eyes. As angry as he made her, he was half-right. Johnny didn't deserve a second chance, but she couldn't keep Jack from his father. She wanted to spare her son any pain, too, but that was not always possible. Taking a deep, shuddering breath, she wiped her tears away with both hands and dried her fingers on her apron. When she went back inside the bar, her father put his arm over her shoulder and ushered her aside.

"What did he have to say for himself?"

Mimi smiled shakily. "He wants to see Jack."

George's eyes narrowed and his jaw tensed. "What did you tell him?"

"That I'd think about it."

"Why now? After all these years?"

Mimi shrugged. "I doubt Johnny could answer that question." Keeping her voice low, she added, "But he is Jack's father. Do I have the right to keep them apart?"

"You do if it's the right thing for Jack," George said gruffly. "The boy's just gotten his feet under him. I don't want to see that fall apart."

"I know." Mimi sighed. "I have to think about it, Dad."

George squeezed her shoulder affectionately. "You'll make the right decision. If you want to talk about it, I'm here."

"I know." With a smile of gratitude, Mimi nodded. "You want to get out of here? I can handle things."

"You sure? You're the one who needs the privacy."

"No, I need the distraction. Go on. I think Mom had a surprise for you at the house."

"A surprise? What?"

"If I told you, it wouldn't be a surprise."

"You sure?" George took his arm from her shoulders reluctantly. "Call if you need anything."

She loved her father so much at that moment. She could not imagine growing up without him. Jack deserved the same love and support, but she could not imagine Johnny Sinclair being that kind of father. Perhaps the best thing Johnny had done for Jack was walking away all those years ago, though she hadn't thought so at the time.

If she could pick a father for Jack, it would be Ian Berzani. She knew in her heart that Jack would, too. But he was leaving. And Johnny had returned asking for a second chance. Mimi wiped another tear from the corner of her eye. Between the two men, there was no choice at all.

IAN TRIED WITH LITTLE SUCCESS to forget his revelation of Thursday afternoon. He didn't want to be in love with Mimi Green, so he wouldn't be—even if he had to rip out his own heart to make it true. Jack made no appearance on Friday and, while Ian missed the boy, it avoided another possible encounter with Mimi. Saturday morning Jack showed up for sailing class, greeting Ian with a happy grin.

No longer the scowling kid with an oversize chip on his shoulder, Jack was making friends with the other kids. He and two other boys already competed to see who could sail the fastest, turn the quickest and tip a boat the farthest without flipping it. He crowed to Ian about a perfect score on his math test and a field trip his class was taking to the Air and Space Museum in D.C. next week. He was swiftly becoming a happy, well-adjusted kid.

After class, Ian turned to Jack. "You want to come up to the shop and work on your boat?"

"I can't," Jack said in a grumble. "I'm grounded until Monday."

"Ouch!" Patrick said, a twinkle of amusement in his eyes. "What'd you get caught doing?"

"I came over here to see Ian when I wasn't supposed to."

"Bummer. Your mom's a tough one," Evan said with a chuckle.

"It's not fair," Jack said with a huff of air. "I only had one page of math to do. *One*." He looked up at the three men to confirm the ridiculousness of the punishment.

"Life isn't fair," Evan said, ruffling Jack's hair. "If it's any comfort to you, we're in the same boat."

"You grounded, too?" Ian asked.

"I might as well be," Evan said with a grimace. "I promised Kippy I'd go to a barbecue at her brother's house. It's his birthday."

"Better you than me," Ian said, then turned to Jack. "Are we still sailing tomorrow?"

"Yeah, but I don't get to do anything else," Jack said gloomily.

"I know the feeling," Evan said. "Come on, kid. I'll give you a ride home." He raised a hand in farewell to Patrick and Ian. "I'll catch you later."

Jack followed Evan up the dock, then turned and ran back. "Can my mom come, too?"

Ian froze. He looked down into Jack's face and felt torn in two directions. He so much wanted to see Mimi, especially after brooding about her for the past two days. But the three of them together on his boat felt like a dangerous idea. Still, he couldn't bring himself to deny Jack.

"Okay," he said slowly. "If you want her to."

"Maybe it would make her happy."

Ian frowned. "Is she sad?"

Jack shrugged. "Grandpop says she is."

"Then we should try to cheer her up." Ian barely restrained the urge to go check on Mimi himself. Tomorrow would have to be soon enough.

"Cool!" Jack grinned and ran off to catch up with Evan.

Patrick looked at his brother and sighed. "I told you your plan stunk."

"What plan?"

"Keeping your distance? Hands to yourself?" Patrick asked with a grin. "Does any of that sound familiar?"

"If you mean Mimi, she and I have an understanding."

"What exactly do you understand?" Patrick narrowed his eyes as he stared at his brother. "I see her around the yard a lot," he added softly.

Ian glared for a moment, then raked a hand through his hair. "Shit."

Patrick pointed to a dock box behind him. "Have a seat. I think we need to talk."

Ian sat as ordered, and his brother joined him. Ian stared down at his hands in silence. Finally, he looked over at Patrick. "How do you know if you're in love?"

"Well, there are the classic symptoms. Do you want to be with her all the time? Does your brain stop functioning when she's close enough to kiss? Do you have trouble sleeping, eating or drinking when she's *not* around?" Patrick had stretched his legs out as he ticked off the questions on the fingers of one hand. He looked at Ian, one eyebrow raised. "Stop me if I'm getting warm."

"Shit," Ian repeated, rubbing both hands over his face. "What do I do now?"

"You've got the same two choices you had before—stay or go."

"And both of them still suck." Ian sighed. "So my case is hopeless."

"Not necessarily." Patrick put his hands on his knees. "Which matters more, Ian? Being with her or having your dream?"

Ian looked out over the water. Which *did* matter more? His head and his heart were split in a tug-of-war that neither could win. He glanced over at his brother. "Sometimes, you're no help at all."

Patrick laughed and stood up. "Maybe not. But if there's cold beer on your boat, I can at least help you drink it."

He held out his hand. Ian looked at him for a moment, then took the hand and let Patrick pull him to his feet. Together, they walked down the dock. Ian still had a decision to make. What it would be, he didn't know. And if he didn't choose, time would do the job for him, of that much he was sure.

Chapter Twelve

A sluggish breeze out of the southwest caught the spinnaker and filled it with a pop. The bright blue, green and yellow stripes dazzled the eye as the sun filtered through the thin, translucent fabric. Ian held the line that was wrapped around the starboard winch.

"Crank the sheet in a little, runt. Let's see if we can hold this course."

Jack grabbed the winch handle and turned it slowly, drawing the sail back. "How far?"

"A little more." Ian watched the sail start to flutter. "That'll do it."

The boat settled into a steady glide as the sail pulled her across the rippled surface. Lines creaked, the wind shifted slightly and the sail fluttered on the edge of collapse. Mimi glanced at the telltales and corrected the wheel. The fabric ballooned again and steadied. Ian cleated the line he held, coiled it and dropped it into a neat pile on the cockpit seat. Copying him, Jack did the same for the line on the opposite winch.

The cockpit was small and horseshoe shaped. The wheel pedestal where Mimi stood was bolted into the back third of the well and took up most of the floor space. The wood seats that lined the perimeter had a curved combing around the outside for a backrest.

"You never told me that you knew how to sail." Ian leaned back to watch Mimi.

"You never asked." She grinned, happy to be aboard *Minerva* with her son and Ian.

Jack dropped down onto the seat behind her. "Yeah, Mom. You're good at this."

"I still have a few surprises left in me."

"When'd you learn how to sail?" Jack asked.

"The first time? When I was about your age," Mimi said, keeping her eyes on the sail and the surrounding water. "Your grandpop had a Sunfish and we'd go out and sail on the creek. We ended up capsizing it about half the time." She laughed at the memory. "He was teaching himself at the same time he was teaching me."

Ian chuckled. "Sounds like me and Patty. I think we did more swimming than sailing the first summer."

"I haven't tipped over once," Jack said proudly.

"Maybe you're not trying hard enough," Ian said, tipping his sunglasses down to wink at the boy.

"Don't encourage him," Mimi said sternly. She saw Jack's grin of delight at the idea of capsizing a boat.

"C'mon, Mom," he said. "You did it, so why can't I?"

Mimi pursed her lips. "That is *never* going to be a good excuse for you to do anything." She looked down at him and shook her finger. "Learn from my mistakes, kiddo."

Jack smirked as if the possibilities were rolling around his head already. Ian went down the companionway steps, disappearing into the cabin for a few minutes. When he reappeared, he had soft drinks, a bowl of chips and a bag of mixed nuts and dried fruit. He handed cans to Jack and Mimi, then passed the snacks.

"If you get tired of steering, just say the word," he told Mimi.

The wind had picked up slightly and the sail was

billowing gently in the breeze. *Minerva* picked up her skirts and sped over the light chop. "I'm enjoying this. But I don't want to have all the fun. Do you want to take over?"

"Not especially." Ian looked over at Jack. "But someone else looks ready to give it a try."

Jack bounced to his feet. "You bet!"

Mimi stepped away as soon as her son had his hands on the wheel. Ian gave directions, telling Jack how to point the boat so that the wind filled the spinnaker. Jack wore a stern look of concentration as he tried to follow Ian's instructions. Taking her soda, Mimi climbed around Jack and sat forward of the wheel.

Watching the two work together, she felt a wash of joy rush through her. Life was wonderful right at this moment. The sun was shining, there was a breeze blowing and she had the two males she loved right beside her. If only she could have them here forever. Ian looked at her and she gave him a slight smile, glad her eyes were shaded by the dark glasses she wore. Too much would be revealed if she took them off.

"Thanks for inviting me."

Ian nodded. "My pleasure."

He was silent after that and Mimi didn't know what to say. There was something different about Ian today, some change she couldn't puzzle out. Ever since their almost lovemaking, he had been friendly but distant, keeping his eyes on Jack and averting them from her. Today, she felt an easing of his aloofness. She wished she could see behind *his* sunglasses, while preserving her own defenses.

"How's it going there, runt?" Ian asked as he looked up to check the sails.

"Great! I'm keeping the wind right where you said it should be."

"You're doing a fine job." Ian stood and looked around

the water, then at the chart. "We're getting a little close to that shoal, so let's jibe."

A flurry of activity followed. Mimi took the helm again. Ian dropped the whisker pole and moved it to the other side of the boat. Jack and Mimi let one side of the sail out and drew the other in, setting it on the opposite side. After a few flaps and snaps of fabric as the boat settled into the new point of sail, they were once more coasting along in the water.

"I want to drive some more. Can I?" Jack asked as soon as the spinnaker was drawing the boat on a new course.

Ian shrugged. "Fine by me, but let us know when you get tired."

Mimi again surrendered her post to her son. The afternoon was steamy. Sitting down, she pushed her hair back from her forehead, feeling the sweat bead on her skin. She raised her face to catch a bit of the breeze. Ian took his place opposite her, picking up his can of soda and taking a long drink. He leaned back against the coaming and stretched out, his leg sliding against hers.

For a moment, they stayed that way, then Ian shifted away. A wave of heat washed over Mimi that had nothing to do with the sun or the warm day. They hadn't touched since that long-ago night, and this light contact was unbearably tantalizing. His face was unreadable, but his jaw was tense. Perhaps he was remembering the same thing. When he turned his head and scanned the water ahead of them, she let out the breath she hadn't known she was holding.

"I can't imagine being alone on the ocean, sailing like this," she said, trying to remember that he was leaving all too soon.

"It's the most awe-inspiring, beautiful experience. I don't know how to describe it."

"You're going to have a fantastic time," she said, trying

to be supportive. She could give him that, at least. "Do you have a route mapped out?"

"Sort of. I'm going south, then west," he said with a laugh.

"Sounds like a plan."

"No, it's no plan at all and that's the point. I don't care where I go or how long it takes me to get there." He shrugged. "I'm just going to go west until it's east again."

Mimi cocked her head. "Where does west become east?"

Ian smiled a little. "I don't know. I guess I'll find out."

"I wanna go, too, but Mom says I can't," Jack said.

"I'm going to be thousands of miles away by the time summer rolls around next year."

Jack frowned as he absorbed this information. "Next summer? You mean a whole year away?"

The spinnaker snapped as the fabric crumpled in on itself. Ian grabbed the wheel and turned it a bit more to port. "Watch it there, runt. We don't want to wrap the sail around the forestay."

"But you're coming back," Jack said, his tone urgent. Mimi glanced sharply at him, sensing something was amiss.

"Of course. Eventually," Ian said. "But it'll be a couple of years. Three or four, if I can stretch it."

Jack's eyes were glued to Ian's face. His hands, knuckles white, gripped the wheel. "You said you were going to sail around the world. You never said you were going away forever."

"It's not forever, runt." Ian pushed his sunglasses up on top of his head. His brows furrowed and his eyes held a wealth of concern mixed with confusion.

Mimi scooted closer to Jack, perching herself on the top

of the coaming, and put a hand on his shoulder. "What's wrong, Jacky?"

"You said you were my friend," Jack said shrilly, ignoring his mother.

"I *am*." Ian looked first at Jack then to Mimi for help.

"You are not!" Jack shouted, turning the wheel as hard as he could. *Minerva* spun to windward. With a soft whoosh, the sail slewed first to one side, then to the other, before collapsing into a shapeless wad, twisting in on itself, onto the forestay.

"Jack, wait a minute!"

Ignoring Mimi's cry, he pushed past his mother and darted down the companionway steps, disappearing into the cabin. Ian pulled on one line while turning the boat back downwind. He muttered a soft curse as the spinnaker remained twisted into an hourglass shape.

"It's wrapped," he said with a sigh. "I'll have to try to undo it before it gets worse."

"I'll go talk to Jack," Mimi said, turning for the hatch.

Ian stopped her with a touch of his hand. "What the hell just happened?"

"I don't know," she said, just as puzzled. "He knew you were leaving."

Ian's brow wrinkled. "Yeah. We talked about it a couple of times. He's asked me questions about it, too."

"Can you handle the boat by yourself?"

"Sure. But I just don't get it."

"Let me go talk to him, okay?"

Mimi went down into the cabin. Pulling off her sunglasses, she let her eyes adjust to the dim interior for a minute. Jack was not in the main saloon. Poking aft into the quarter berth, she saw only stacked sails and a couple of life jackets. Mimi found him in the forepeak, as far forward as he could get, his back to the anchor locker, knees drawn up to his chest and his head bowed. At the foot of the bed, the overhead was only two feet above the cushions.

He didn't look up as she crawled into the berth with him. Propped on one elbow, she laid a hand on his leg and slowly stroked from ankle to knee for a few minutes. She could hear Ian's footsteps above her head as he struggled with the spinnaker on the foredeck.

"You *knew* Ian was leaving, Jack," she finally said, keeping her tone gentle.

"Not forever." He had buried his face in his arms. His voice was muffled and hard to hear.

"Oh, sweetheart, he *isn't* going forever." Mimi's heart broke for him as she realized that Jack had not grasped how far Ian's dreams would take him from them.

"He won't come back," Jack said, his voice stronger now.

"Yes, he will." She squeezed his leg. "You can keep in touch by e-mail and phone calls. Maybe we can meet him someplace," she added, not knowing if it was possible or even probable.

"I want him to stay."

She stroked his leg again. "So do I, honey, but this is something that Ian has to do. He's dreamed about this journey for so long that it's become a part of who he is. Does that make any sense?"

Mimi waited patiently for a reply. Jack refused to look at her or say more. Finally, she heard him sniff. He uncoiled from his ball and Mimi caught a glimpse of his red, tear-filled eyes before he launched himself into her arms. She fell back on the bed, hugging him tightly as she felt the sobs shake his thin body.

"I hate him," Jack said, his words muffled in her shoulder.

"Oh, Jacky," she said, her heart hurting for him. "No, you don't."

"I do so," he said fiercely.

His weeping increased and tears soaked her shirt. Mimi knew that reasoning with him was hopeless. She held him close as she rubbed a hand in circles on his back. Tears filled her eyes as she held tight to her son, but she didn't let them fall. Jack was crying enough for both of them.

AFTER SETTING THE AUTOPILOT, Ian went forward to free the spinnaker. With a few careful tugs, he gradually coaxed the thin nylon from the forestay. Once free it billowed like a balloon and began pulling *Minerva* forward again. The joy in sailing was gone now and he decided to take the sail down. As he lowered and bagged the spinnaker, Ian's mind turned one question over and over: how had such a sweet day turned so sour?

As usual, it had been a joy to teach Jack and watch him learn. Having Mimi aboard more than doubled the pleasure, especially finding out that she knew how to sail. The sight of her behind *Minerva*'s wheel had taken Ian's breath away. She was perfect for him, in ways he was only beginning to fathom. The fit between the three of them had been seamless, until Jack had gotten so upset. Ian couldn't understand why. The boy knew he was leaving; they had talked about it. Why had Jack suddenly come unhinged?

Sails down, the boat drifted with the current. Ian poked his head down below. He saw no one in the saloon, but he heard something that sounded like crying. Heart pounding, he followed the sound forward. He found Mimi in the v-berth, her eyes closed as she rubbed Jack's back. The boy was cuddled against her, his face hidden. As Ian took a step forward, Mimi's eyes opened and met his. The sadness in them made his muscles clench. Ian reached out a hand to console Jack, but Mimi shook her head. Swallowing hard, he pulled back slowly, turned around and retraced his steps.

In the cockpit, Ian sat for a long while. His head spun and his stomach tangled in knots. Something had gone very wrong today, but he didn't know how to fix it. Finally, he forced himself to work. The wind had died completely and the afternoon heat was stifling. Starting the diesel engine, he steered the boat toward the marina. Neither Mimi nor Jack joined him in the cockpit.

Minerva slid into her slip gracefully. Ian jumped on the dock to secure the mooring lines and then reboarded the boat to turn off the engine. As he was securing the canvas cover over the mainsail, mother and son climbed out of the cabin. Jack's head was down and he didn't look at Ian.

Ian came to the side deck and put a hand on Jack's shoulder. "I'm sorry. For whatever I said that hurt you."

Jack shrugged it off and kept his face averted. He climbed off the boat in silence, his back to Ian.

"We'll be okay," Mimi said. She looked as if she had been crying, but slipped on her sunglasses before he could be certain.

Ian touched her on the arm, wanting to soothe her tears as he had once before. She smiled at him, a twist of her lips that held no happiness.

"I'll walk you back," Ian offered.

"You don't have to."

"Please. I want to," Ian said. He moved past her and jumped off the boat. Turning, he reached to help her down the boarding steps. She took his hand for a moment, steadying herself, then dropped it. Silently, they walked up the dock, Jack a few paces ahead of them.

"Jack, will you forgive me?" Ian asked, without knowing exactly what he had done wrong. When they reached land,

Jack had still not turned or acknowledged Ian. "Come on, runt," he said. "We're friends. Tell me what's wrong."

No answer. Ian shot a glance at Mimi, who shrugged her shoulders a little. Ian felt frustration rise. He could not mend what Jack kept hidden.

When they reached the main gate, Jack finally turned his head and glared up at Ian. It had been a long time since Ian had seen that glower of insolence on the boy's face. It surprised him.

"I don't want to be your friend," Jack said angrily. "I hate you!" With that, he took off running down the street toward the Laughing Gull and home.

"What the hell is this about?" Ian asked, more bewildered than angry. He turned to Mimi. "What did I do?"

Mimi bit her lip. "He doesn't mean it, Ian. He's just hurt."

"Because I'm leaving in a couple of months? But he *knew* that."

Mimi pulled off her sunglasses and looked at him with sad eyes. "No, he didn't. Not really. Maybe he didn't *want* to understand. I don't know." She sighed. "Anyway, he gets it now and it hurts. He feels betrayed."

"But we talked about my plans, all the places I want to see and how big the Pacific Ocean is," he said urgently, wanting her to believe him.

Mimi nodded. "I know you didn't deceive him. It's just—" She stopped and bit her lip. Ian saw her blink rapidly, as if she was holding back tears.

"What?"

"You're his best friend," she said softly. "His *only* friend, really. Now he's going to lose you."

"I thought he knew," Ian said on a sigh of regret. "Damn."

"I know." They were both silent, looking up the street.

She turned back to face him. "He wouldn't say much to me. I'll see if I can get him to talk about it tonight."

"If there's any way I can make it up to him, I'll do it," Ian said. He ran a hand over his head, raking his hair back. "I *am* sorry, Mimi. I would never hurt Jack."

"I know," she repeated. "Give him some time. He's only nine, even though I forget that sometimes." Her lips curved in a wry smile. "He'll come around."

Ian stuck his hands in his pockets. "I hope you're right."

"Thanks for the sail."

"You're welcome," he said with a shrug. "I guess."

"I'll see you later, then."

Ian watched her walk away. When she was out of sight, he turned and went back to *Minerva*. Sitting in the cockpit, he dropped his head into his hands. He had tried so hard to be fair to everyone, but he had still wounded Jack. Maybe Mimi was right: the kid hadn't wanted to believe the truth. He heard what he wanted and ignored the rest until it smacked him in the face.

As Ian thought it over, he realized that something had smacked him, too. He had been congratulating himself for handling Jack so well, seeing things in the boy that even his mother had missed. He had befriended the boy, taught him to sail, to respect his mother's wishes, even to excel in school. He relished the bond he and Jack had forged.

On top of that, he had fallen in love with Jack's mother. He stole whatever time he could with Mimi, kissed her, touched her, desired her in ways he had never desired a woman before. Did he really think that he could be Jack's buddy and Mimi's lover one day and just sail off into the blue the next? They would stand on the dock waving him a fond farewell, a painless departure for all, even for himself?

No. He had deceived himself just as much as Jack had.

Ian rubbed his hands over his face, then took a long, loving look at the boat he had made with his own two hands. Her strong hull and stout rig could carry him and all his worldly belongings across the oceans of the world. He had built her to handle all of his hopes and dreams, as well. Almost all, anyway. He had not foreseen that a surly young boy and a beautiful woman would invade his dreams, changing them so that they would no longer fit so neatly in one thirty-six-foot package.

Gazing at *Minerva* and all her details that he had so carefully crafted, Ian knew he would not be going anywhere for a long time. He would stay in Crab Creek. The truth was all too clear. He could not ignore it any more than Jack could. He knew how to fix Jack's broken heart. Jack needed him. Maybe Mimi did, too. Mostly though, Ian needed them. He might regret staying, but right now he knew he would regret leaving even more.

Chapter Thirteen

As she walked home, Mimi felt Ian's eyes on her every step of the way. When she reached the Laughing Gull, she considered stopping and telling her father about Jack's heartbreak and hearing his advice. She could see that the bar was packed, though. The Orioles were playing today; the Gull usually had a crowd on game days. She continued to the house and entered through the kitchen door. From the refrigerator, she took out a pitcher of iced tea and poured herself a large glass. As she took the first sip, Claire came in from the hall.

"What's wrong with Jack?" her mother asked. "He slammed through here like a scalded cat. When I followed him upstairs to see what was wrong, he refused to talk to me."

"He's upset with Ian," Mimi said with a sigh.

"With Ian?" Claire blinked in astonishment. "That's impossible!"

Mimi closed her eyes and ran the cool glass over her forehead. "He just found out how long Ian will be gone on his sailing adventure."

"He knows that." Claire frowned. "*Every*one knows that."

Shaking her head, Mimi related all that had happened that afternoon as she slid into a chair at the table. Claire sat down across from her. Putting a hand over her mouth, the older woman slowly shook her head in dismay.

"Oh, my. No wonder he's upset."

"Yeah." Mimi took a long drink from her glass. Setting it down, she rose. "I'd better go talk to him."

"Good luck, dear."

Upstairs, Mimi knocked softly on Jack's door. Getting no response, she turned the knob and eased it open. At least it wasn't locked. She expected to see Jack curled up on the bed crying. He was on the bed, but he was thumbing the buttons on a handheld video game, his eyes intent on some electronic battle.

"Hey," Mimi said. "Can we talk?"

Jack flashed a glance at her, then back to his game. He shook his head. Mimi walked over and sat on the end of the bed anyway. She toyed with the laces of his shoes.

"Ian's really sorry, Jack. He didn't mean to hurt your feelings." She watched his face. His lips pursed at the mention of Ian's name, but he kept punching buttons at the same frenetic pace. "Come on," she said, wiggling his foot. "What's going on in there?"

Jack put the game down, but remained silent. Mimi waited for a while, then she shook his foot again. "Jack?"

"You said it would be different." He picked at some loose thread on the bedspread, keeping his lashes lowered.

"*What* would be different?"

His eyes met hers, fiercely blue and accusing. "You said if we came to Crab Creek I'd make friends and I'd have them for the *rest* of my *life*."

"Oh, Jacky." Mimi swiveled, drawing one leg up under her. "I didn't say that exactly."

"You lied!"

"No, I didn't. You *will* make friends here, ones that you'll know for a long, long time."

"Ian's leaving in October. That's not a *long* time."

So he was furious with her now, as well as Ian. All his pain had transferred itself into anger, unleashed on the nearest target. Mimi could tell by the way his lower lip stuck out that Jack was done listening. There would be no reasoning with him. He would have a counterargument for everything she said. Yes, she *had* promised him a permanent home, with friends he didn't have to leave after a few months. How could she have known his best friend would leave *him?* She sighed.

"I'm sorry. I didn't lie to you, even though you don't want to believe that."

Jack shrugged and looked away across the room.

Mimi rose to her feet. "We'll talk later."

Leaving the room, she closed the door behind her quietly. When she got to the bottom of the stairs, Claire met her there.

"Well?"

"I've been outwitted by a nine-year-old once again."

"Which means what?"

"It's my fault Jack is unhappy."

"I thought it was Ian's."

"His, too. Ian gets the blame for leaving and I catch it for promising Jack that he would make *permanent* friends when we settled here."

Understanding dawned on Claire's face. "Oh."

"He's not open to other explanations right now," Mimi said, rubbing a hand over her forehead. "I'll try again later."

"Is there something I can do?"

Before Mimi could think of anything, the doorbell rang.

"Maybe that's Ian." She went to the door, opened it and gasped.

There on the doorstep stood Johnny Sinclair. "Hey, beautiful. I was in the neighborhood. Can I come in?"

Mimi scowled at him, thinking that, as usual, Johnny's timing was either very bad or very good. At the moment, she was not sure which.

IAN CONVINCED HIMSELF that he should wait. There was no rush to announce his decision. Jack needed time to cool down. Mimi needed time to talk to her son. Ian himself needed to think carefully, to be certain that he was doing what was right for all three of them. And Ian did his best thinking when his hands had something to occupy them.

He tried puttering on *Minerva:* the decks could use a scrub, the rigging could be tuned, the end of the main halyard needed to be whipped, and a long list of other chores and tasks. Yet he already felt detached from his boat, as if working on her was now pointless. None of the sixty-two items on his to-do list needed to be done any time soon. They could wait.

Even though it was Sunday, he decided the wood shop would offer something more soothing. He unlocked the door and turned on the fan to blow out the hot, stuffy air. None of the three jobs he had yet to complete appealed to him. He didn't want to build a new hatch for a sailboat, a set of drawers for a trawler or a pin rail for an old schooner.

Instead, he got out his best chisels from the tool drawer, lining all twenty of them out on the workbench. Then he oiled a whetstone. One at a time he began to sharpen the tips. He made a deal with himself. When all the chisels were sharpened—if he was still sure—he would go talk to Mimi and tell her that he had decided to stay.

The job took just over two hours. The rubbing of steel on

oiled stone was exactly the sort of mindful, yet mindless, project he needed to gather his scattered wits. As each tip became razor sharp, Ian's focus sharpened, too. By the time he turned off the lights and the fans, he was certain he was doing the right thing.

He stepped outside, locking the door to the shop behind him. The sun had disappeared and a breeze had picked up off the water. A large moon hung in the eastern sky. *A perfect evening for a sail,* he thought. But he had other business tonight. Hands in his pockets, Ian started down the street for the Laughing Gull.

George greeted him when he stepped through the door of the Gull and asked about Mimi. "Haven't seen her since this morning. She's probably over at the house."

When Ian knocked on the front door, Claire Green answered.

"Ian! What a surprise, come in."

"I hope I'm not intruding." Ian took two steps inside and closed the door behind him.

"No, not at all," she said with a smile, but her eyes darted away toward the voices that came from the back of the house.

Unexpectedly, Ian heard Jack's familiar giggle followed by Mimi's husky laugh. He was startled to hear them so happy. A kernel of uncertainty formed in the pit of Ian's stomach. Then a third voice—a man's laughter—rang out above the other two.

His jaw tensed, but he forced a polite smile to his lips. "You have company."

The older woman frowned. "Well, yes, we do, but that—"

"I'll come back another time."

Before he could escape, Mimi appeared in the doorway

to the left, her face flushed with laughter. "Ian? I thought that might be you."

"I came to check on Jack," he said, keeping his voice even by sheer force of will. "But he sounds like he's fine."

"He's found a distraction anyway," Mimi said.

Claire looked between them, then backed away. "I'll just leave you alone," she murmured.

"No. Don't," he told the older woman, his tone hard. "I've got to go."

His words didn't stop Claire; she slipped past her daughter and out of the room. As she left, Ian kept his gaze on Mimi. Her smile faded and a puzzled look came into her eyes. Ian shook his head, unwilling to say another word. Not now. Putting his hand on the doorknob, he twisted it just as Mimi wrapped her fingers around his wrist.

"Ian, wait. What are you so angry about?" Mimi asked, frowning.

He stared at the door panel for a moment, then turned to her. "I was worried about Jack. And you. So I came over to talk to you both," he said tightly. "Obviously, it was unnecessary."

Ian yanked at the door, but Mimi leaned against it, keeping him from leaving.

"I'm sorry, Ian. I didn't think," she said softly. "We had an unexpected guest and I didn't call you."

"Mimsy, come on," a man's voice called from another room. "Where's your guitar? Jack wants to hear us sing another song."

A tall, lean form in a blue chambray shirt, jeans and boots appeared in the doorway where Claire had disappeared. At the same time, Ian felt Mimi's hand tense, then she snatched it away from his arm. The stranger seemed familiar, but Ian couldn't place where he had seen him before.

"Fantastic," the man said with a smile. "An audience."

"Tell Jack to get my guitar out of the closet," Mimi said. "I'll be there in a second."

"Aren't you going to introduce me to your friend?" the man asked, cocking his head to one side. When Mimi hesitated, the man held out a hand to Ian. "Johnny Sinclair."

The name was instantly recognizable. In other circumstances, Ian might even be impressed to find a rock star in the Green house. As it was, a few more pieces fell into place, making the picture clearer, but no prettier.

"Ian Berzani," he said tersely as they shook hands.

Mimi looked even more uncomfortable. "Go entertain Jack. I'll be with you in a minute," she said to Johnny.

The other man didn't move, standing and looking back and forth between them, speculation in his eyes. "Mimi and I were just reworking some old material," he said with a slight smile. "It's been too long since we've played together."

Ian stiffened and said nothing. A gauntlet had just been thrown, invisible, but palpable. Narrowly eyeing the man, Ian considered—and rejected—responding to it. He shot a glance at Mimi, but her eyes would not meet his. Then Jack ran into the room. The boy stopped short when he saw Ian.

"Hey, runt," Ian said. "How's it going?"

Jack stared at him, the light in his face slowly dying and a scowl replacing it. He said nothing, in fact seemed to choose at that moment to ignore Ian. Turning to Johnny, Jack grinned. "Want to come upstairs and see my posters? I got one of you and the band." Taking Johnny's hand, he tugged at him.

With a laugh, Johnny followed. He looked back at Mimi. "Looks like I can't refuse."

Ian looked from the boy to the man and registered the identical smiles, the same face shape. As he watched them run up the stairs together, he felt as if he had been punched in the stomach. They disappeared at the top, but the echo of their laughter rang down. It seemed as though they were laughing at him. He swallowed hard and turned to look at Mimi.

"Jack's father?" he asked, his voice just above a whisper.

Mimi's eyes widened and she shot a worried glance up the stairs. She nodded and bit her lip. Closing his eyes, Ian absorbed the truth—for the second time today. His anger had faded under the force of astonishment. When he opened his eyes again, Mimi was watching him, a glint of fear in her gaze.

"Please don't say anything, I—"

"No." Ian shook his head, whether to answer her plea or to clear his fogged thoughts, he didn't know. He saw some of the tension in her shoulders ease as he spoke. "I won't. Why would I?"

"He showed up after I got back. Jack was so upset and he loves Johnny's music, so I just—I thought it would help."

"Of course." He looked back up the stairs, then over at Mimi. "I didn't realize you were in contact with Jack's father."

"I haven't been," she said softly. "He came by the Gull the other day and—" Her eyes pleaded with him to understand. "He asked to see Jack. To get to know him."

A visceral urge to protect rose inside Ian. "So, just like that," he said, snapping his fingers, "you let him back in Jack's life."

She darted a glance up the stairs, then stepped closer. "He *is* Jack's father—"

"Right. And he's been missing for how long now? Nine years?" Ian asked, keeping his own voice low, his eyes locked on Mimi's. "It's been so long that Jack told me he doesn't *have* a dad."

Her eyes widened. "He said that to you?"

"Yeah. Once."

"He never talks about it to me." Mimi rubbed her hands over her arms, as if chilled.

"I didn't have any idea what to say to him, how to answer his questions. Not that he had any then," Ian said with a laugh that held no mirth. "Of course, now he has all his answers, here in the flesh."

"Look, I never want Jack to be hurt, Ian. *Never.* But Johnny is his father and if he wants to be part of Jack's life…" She paused, biting her lip. "He *needs* a man in his life."

Ian jerked as if he had been slapped. "And that's not going to be me."

"No. You're *leaving.*" Tears flooded Mimi's eyes and her voice cracked. "It wasn't until I saw Jack with you that I realized how much he's needed a father. I want him to have that, that…bond with another man. Someone who will take an interest in him, like you have. Be more than a friend to him," she finished softly.

"And who better than his own father," Ian said flatly.

Again, voices, one low and one high with excitement, drifted down the stairs, getting louder with each word.

"We can't talk about this here," Mimi said, wiping the tears from her lashes.

Staring into Mimi's troubled eyes for a long moment, Ian took a deep breath. Jack's sneakered feet sounded on the stairs, followed by a pair of leather boots. She was right. They couldn't talk here. Really, they couldn't talk *anywhere*. There was nothing to say.

Everything had become clear in a minute. Johnny Sinclair was Jack's real father and if he wanted a second chance to fill those shoes, Mimi would give it to him. Not because he deserved it, but because Jack deserved it. Stuffing all the words he wanted to say—all the protests he wanted to make—deep inside, Ian turned away and pulled open the door.

Mimi followed him outside, as far as the front steps. "I tried to talk to Jack earlier, Ian, but he wouldn't listen. He's just as mad at *me* as he is at you."

"Leave the kid alone. He's got work to do with his father," Ian said. "If he wants to see me, he knows where to find me."

"But you're his friend, too. And mine."

"I won't be around much longer, Mimi. Better we just forget about it and move on."

Mimi bit her lip. She looked down, her arms still crossed tightly. Unable to stop himself, Ian reached up and brushed his fingers across her cheek. Her eyes rose and he could see tears shining in them again. He wished he could hold her, kiss her, but that would only prolong the pain of admitting it was over. Instead, Ian dropped his hand from her cheek, squared his shoulders and walked down the steps and across the sidewalk. As he did, he heard Jack's joyful laughter peal from an open window.

As the darkness swallowed him, Ian thought that he ought to be glad for the kid. Every boy deserved a father. Tucking his hands in his pockets, he took a gulp of night air. He ought to feel happy for himself, too. He could sail off on *Minerva* and pursue his dreams without worry or guilt. Nothing tied him to land anymore, *nothing*. Too bad those dreams tasted so bitter now.

Chapter Fourteen

Someone knocked on *Minerva's* hull. Ian ignored it. He had his head stuck in a starboard locker, counting cans of soup. He closed the lid of the bin and wrote 23 on the manifest, next to Soup Cans. The pounding sounded again, louder this time.

"Ian! Are you in there?" Patrick's shout was quickly followed by the thud of footsteps on the deck as he stepped on board. He came to the companionway and crouched down, looking inside the cabin. "You hiding from me?"

"I'm busy." Ian continued to check his list. "Go away."

Patrick ignored the order and climbed down the steps. "Jeez, looks like a bomb went off in here."

Piles of gear were heaped on the floor, the table, the settees and nav desk: charts, bosun's chair, extra rope, a sea anchor, cans of food, bags of pasta and rice. Nearly every locker was open. Ian sifted through a heap of food in plastic bags on the table, then stuffed as many of the bags as would fit in a locker, counting as he went.

Patrick, who could go no farther into the cabin than two feet, perched on the steps, his elbows on his knees. "Ma says you're leaving."

"Our mother, she sure likes to start rumors."

"A bit ahead of schedule, aren't you?"

"Plans change." Ian refused to look at his brother.

"In case you hadn't noticed, it's still hurricane season."

Ian shrugged and opened another locker, stowing the bosun's chair along the side and laying coils of rope next to it. The spare main halyard fit on top. "I thought I'd head up to Maine until the end of October. I'll go direct to Bermuda from there."

"I don't suppose this has anything to do with Mimi?" Patrick asked.

"Who told you that? Ma?"

"No one. I have eyes and I see a man who suddenly can't stand to stick around."

"Congratulations. You're not as dumb as you look."

Patrick sighed. "Come on, Ian. Talk to me."

"Fine. I'll give you the long version—it's over. End of story."

"Last I heard you were in love with her. What happened?"

Closing his eyes, Ian took a deep breath, holding it until the pain in his heart eased. Dropping his tablet on top of the pile on the settee, he turned to his brother. Briefly, he related how Jack had fallen apart on Sunday while they were sailing.

"Remember when you asked me what I wanted more, my dream or her?" Ian shook his head. "I was all set to sail away, you know? Just leave and forget them. After that mess on Sunday, I knew I couldn't. I *knew* what was more important. And it wasn't this boat or my plans."

"So, I don't get it. Why are you leaving?"

Ian fidgeted with his pen, clicking the tip in and out. "Jack's father showed up."

"What?" Patrick's mouth dropped open in surprise. "I thought he was long gone."

"So did everyone else." Ian tossed the pen down. "His

timing is perfect, I'll say that much for him. He shows up just when everything's gone to hell. The hero riding to the rescue. I suppose he spared me from promising that I'd stay and making a fool of myself."

"That still doesn't explain why you're leaving."

"Yeah, Patty, it does." Ian slumped to a seat on a pile of rope. "He wants to be a fixture in Jack's life, and Mimi's going to let him. I can't say she's wrong. A kid needs his father."

"There are a lot of fathers and sons out there who don't share the same blood."

"How would you feel if someone else wanted to replace you and take over fathering Beth?" Ian asked, spearing him with a glance.

"This is different," Patrick said impatiently. "Jack's nine and his father's never been around. The bastard abandoned Mimi and his kid. He lost his chance."

"I agree. But doesn't Jack deserve another chance with the guy if *he* wants it?"

Patrick glared at him, then blew out a breath. "Do you ever think of yourself, Ian? Because it's damn hard hanging around a saint sometimes."

Ian laughed a little, despite the wave of sadness that had swamped him. "What I want doesn't matter right now. Jack needs—no, the kid *deserves* a father. If his real one wants the job, I won't stand in the way. But to stay here and watch that happen …" He let the words trail off as he shook his head again. "It just hurts too much."

"Is it more painful than leaving?" Patrick asked urgently. "And what about Mimi?"

"She was in love with Jack's father once. If I disappear, those feelings might rekindle."

"And they might not."

Ian shrugged. "I've got to live my own life. I'm not going

to stand on the sidelines and wait for a chance to get in the game."

Patrick looked as if he wanted to argue more, but he kept silent. Ian stood and picked up his tablet again. "So if you'll pardon me, I've got to get the rest of this packed up."

"Need some help?"

"I've seen you pack. No, thanks."

Standing, Patrick half turned to go up the stairs, then stopped. "Once, when I was running away from my problems, you told me that the ocean wasn't going to give me any answers." His eyes searched Ian's. "I don't think it's going to help you, either."

With that warning, Patrick climbed the steps and left the boat. Ian stood in the middle of the cabin for a moment, then turned to the nearest pile of gear. True. Maybe the sea wouldn't give him any answers. But maybe, out there alone, he could forget the questions.

THE STEREO WAS PLAYING some slow, lugubrious ballad of lost love. Mimi couldn't take another note. There was a lull in the patrons haunting the Gull this Thursday afternoon and she needed a song to distract her thoughts, something more cheerful to lift her spirits. She leaned against the cooler, drumming her fingers on the front of it, flipping through her CD choices. A little Kirsty MacColl ought to do it.

As she slipped in her choice, her father walked into the bar, a newspaper tucked under one arm. "Quite a crowd in here, I see."

"It's been like this for over an hour. I was thinking about stretching out on the bar and having a nap."

Her father chuckled. "Go over to the house and do that,

if you like. I'm planning to sit and read the paper. Your mother just got back from picking Jack up at school."

"Did you talk to him?"

"We exchanged a few grunts," George said.

Mimi sighed. "He's not speaking to me at all, so I suppose you could count yourself lucky."

"His mood isn't getting any sunnier."

"Not unless Johnny's hanging around."

"Speaking of which, where is our token celebrity? I haven't seen him today."

"I don't think you will. He's got a concert tonight."

"Well, we get a break at last."

"You don't like him, do you? Every time you look at him you scowl." Mimi looked over at her father. "Mom's edgy around him, too."

"More to the point, I don't trust him." George patted her arm. "I can't figure out what exactly Mr. Sinclair wants. Is he just here to make up with his son after all these years?"

"I don't know. I've been wondering the same thing, to tell you the truth."

George unrolled his newspaper and spread it over the bar. "All I can say is, I liked it better when Jack was hanging out with Ian. I wish they would just kiss and make up."

"I suggested that he go talk to Ian, but that didn't go over very well. Jack's determined to sulk."

"Too bad. I keep hoping that Ian will change his mind and stay."

Chewing on her lip, Mimi silently agreed with her father. She had not seen Ian since Sunday, despite the longing in her heart. He was right: they had no future together. Pretending otherwise just meant more heartache. True to his word, Ian had stayed away so that Jack and Johnny could bond. But the separation hadn't improved Jack's mood. He nursed his wounds so that no one forgot how hurt he was, showing just how much Ian meant to him.

"Actually, maybe I'll run over and talk to Ian. About Jack."

"If you think it will help," George said with a frown.

"He means a lot to Jack. Why can't they be friends, whether Ian's here in Crab Creek or halfway around the world? I think I just need to remind both of them."

"Sounds like a reasonable excuse to me."

"What's that supposed to mean?"

George gave her a wink, then turned to the sports page. "It means that I wish you luck."

When she got to A&E Marine, Mimi first looked in the wood shop. The man there told her Ian was probably on his boat. She went down the dock to the sleek, white sailboat they had sailed on last Sunday. The companionway hatch was wide open and she thought she heard someone moving around inside. She knocked on the deck.

"Go away," a voice commanded.

"Ian?" Mimi peered around the dodger. From the dock, she could see nothing in the dark cabin. "Ian, is that you?"

Ian's head poked out of the hatch. "Oh. Hi. Sorry, I thought it was Patrick."

"Can I come aboard?"

"Sure."

Mimi climbed from the dock onto the side deck and from there into the cockpit. "I think we should talk about— Wow, what's going on here?" She was halfway down the ladder into the cabin when she saw the piles of gear scattered everywhere.

"I'm stocking the boat." His eyes met hers, his dark and fathomless. "I'm leaving next week."

"Oh?" His words hit her with the force of a blow. Mimi felt stunned. "But I thought you weren't going until October," she whispered.

"There seems to be no reason to stick around." He fidgeted with a piece of twine, wrapping it around his fingers. "It's time."

Tears filled her eyes. She blinked furiously to stop them from spilling over, looking anywhere but at Ian. Settling her eyes on the top button of his shirt, she said, "So that's it, then. I don't know what to say. I guess goodbye." Her voice broke on the last word and she turned away before he could see her cry.

"Mimi, I'm sorry—"

She halted, one foot still on the lowest step. "No! Don't say you're sorry. This is your *dream,* Ian." Turning, not caring that he saw tears streaming down her face, she tried to smile. "Follow it and be happy. Please. For me."

"Ah, Mimi." Ian's hands came up to cup her face, his thumbs wiping at her tears. "Don't cry."

"I'm happy for you, I really am. I'll just—" Her voice broke again and she swallowed hard. Her fingers gripped his strong wrists. "We'll miss you."

"I'll miss you, too," he whispered.

Their eyes met—blue to brown—and neither could speak. So much left unspoken over the past weeks could not be said now. Stretching up on tiptoe, Mimi pressed a kiss to Ian's lips. Soft and warm, they molded to hers. His hands dropped to her waist, hers slid around his neck. Angling his head, he took the kiss deeper, seeking and gaining access to the tender inside of her mouth. Mimi sighed as she tasted him once more. Her fingers delved into his soft curls to urge him close and closer still.

Ian obliged her, his arms cinching around her. One held her close while the other hand followed a trail up her spine to cradle her head. The kiss flared from warm to hot in seconds. She wanted more: more taste, more touch, more fire. One last chance. Mimi arched her back and pressed her breasts to his chest, easing the ache there. One leg rose and curled around Ian's. She felt his body rise to hers as his hand dropped to her bottom, then slid along her thigh, lifting her leg higher. When he ground himself against her, Mimi whimpered in pleasure.

"We can't do this," he said against her lips. Yet, even as he spoke, he cupped her breast in the palm of his hand.

Mimi gasped as his thumb brushed the nipple, bringing it to singing life. "Yes, we can. Please, Ian. We won't have another chance." Her fingernails bit into the fabric of his shirt.

"I can't stay." His voice was low and harsh, as he bent his head to bite gently at the turgid peak through the barrier of her clothes.

"I know." The truth was painful, but brought a measure of sanity. Taking a deep breath, she drew his head up so that their eyes could meet, holding his gaze with hers. Mimi saw the war being waged within him. "I won't keep you from going, Ian, but I want this. I want *you.*" She kissed him softly, biting at his lower lip. "Make love to me," she whispered. "Please."

He closed his eyes for a long moment, holding perfectly still. When they opened, the dark depths were filled with a blaze of passion. One hand came up to tangle in her hair as he lowered his mouth to hers once more. The kiss went on and on, taking them deeper and deeper into the reckless fire. The reins of caution had been thrown off. When his lips released hers, blazing a trail of heat down her throat, Mimi groaned.

In seconds, Ian had stripped the T-shirt she wore over her head and flipped open the clasp of her bra. Taking her breasts in his hands, he shaped them eagerly, pinching her nipples and sending a thrill of need straight to her core. Eager to press his skin to hers, Mimi fumbled with the buttons on his shirt. She made little progress, distracted by the kisses he was placing in a line from one nipple to the other. Finally, he reached an arm back and grabbed his shirt, pulling it over his head, ignoring the buttons altogether.

Needing no further encouragement, Mimi smoothed her hands across the warm, muscled skin he had exposed. Soft curling hair tickled the palms of her hands as she spread her fingers wide. She flicked her tongue across one nipple and he groaned. Running her hands over his chest, she slid them around his waist, stepping closer so that they touched, skin to skin. They both gasped.

Ian pulled her closer, kissing her deeply. She felt his hands at the waist of her skirt, unfastening the button and zipper. The fabric slid to her ankles soundlessly. Easing away from her, his gaze traveled over her in a slow, sizzling scrutiny. His hands framed her hips, thumbs teasing the skin just above her panties. Mimi basked in his hot stare as the dark shadow behind the white lace drew his gaze. She swayed toward him, just brushing herself against the erection she could see straining his pants. Seeing his jaw flex, she ran both hands up his chest. She offered her mouth and he took it hungrily.

As they kissed, he lifted her in his arms and carried her a few steps farther into the saloon. Mimi held on to his neck tightly as he cleared the settee of rope, bags of rice and flour in one shove. Dimly she heard the thumps and thuds of gear as it hit the floor. He laid her on the cushions and stood above her.

"You're too beautiful," he said in a rasp as he ran his gaze over her.

"Come show me." Mimi raised her arms and beckoned him. His eyes were black now, blazing with desire. Ian's hands went to his belt buckle and she sat up. "Wait."

Her hands pushed his aside as she took charge of the fastenings. Keeping her eyes locked on his, she slowly released his belt, then pulled the snap open with a pop. Grasping the tab of his zipper, she released it tooth by slow tooth. His erection surged as her knuckles brushed against it. She saw him swallow, his face tense with the effort of standing completely still before her. When the zipper was open, the pants dropped to the floor with a clatter of belt buckle and change.

Still looking up at him, she smoothed her hands around his waist, just above the line of his gray boxer briefs. They fit him like a glove, outlining every inch of his muscular thighs and the arousal he could not hide. Mimi put her thumbs under the elastic band and drew them down and off his hips. His penis sprang free, large and urgent, begging for release. She kissed his hip, then moved a bit closer and kissed again.

Ian gasped and took her shoulders in his hands, pushing her back. "If you keep that up, this is going to be over sooner than we want."

Mimi smiled and let herself be pressed down. She arched up into him as he came to cover her body with his own. His weight against her was exquisite. Cupping one of her breasts, Ian began to kiss her again. His hand slid down her stomach, stroking and teasing a path to the white lace she still wore. When his fingers delved beneath, she gasped and whimpered. The callused touch of his fingers on her most intimate skin was more intense than anything she had ever experienced.

"Please," she sobbed as he brought her to the edge of release.

He deftly stripped off her panties and positioned himself at the entrance to her body. There, he stiffened. "Damn, I need—"

"No." Her nails dug into the skin of his shoulders as he lifted himself away. "I'm on the pill."

He kissed her hard and took her in one silken thrust. When he began moving, she raised her hips to his. She wanted it all, *now,* but Ian wouldn't be rushed to completion. He steadily built the pace so that they were caught in a maelstrom of sensation. Every thrust added to the pleasure and sent her closer to the edge. Her heart was pounding, her breathing a staccato pant. Ian was filling her with his desire, body, heart and soul. When there was room for no more, her world exploded in a blast of pleasure unlike any she had ever felt. Stars danced before her eyes and she cried out, a long keening wail. Ian's call joined with hers and he came to a rest on top of her.

Mimi clutched him to her, feeling the frantic beat of his heart against hers. He rose onto his elbows and pressed his lips to hers in a tender kiss. Brushing the hair away from his face, she felt in her body how much she loved this man. More than she had ever thought possible. And now she had to let him go. She couldn't hold him back. Her heart began to ache again for what was to come, but she had no regrets. She would have this memory. It would have to be enough.

As Ian kissed Mimi and wrapped her warm body to his, his heart slowed to a steady, contented beat. His mind still whirled in the aftermath of pleasure. Sighing, he lifted his head and looked into his lover's eyes. They were a deep navy, full of mysterious depths he wanted to plumb. Flushed with love, she was more beautiful than he had ever imagined her. She brushed her fingers through his hair and he kissed her again, savoring the sweetness of her lips. He wanted to make love to her all over again.

She moved under him and he shifted to the side, taking his weight off her. She ran a fingertip down his nose and over his lips in a delicate caress. "That was wonderful," she said quietly.

He nipped at her finger. "And more than that."

Unable to resist, he leaned down and kissed her again. Thankfully, on the narrow settee, he had to lie pressed up against her. He smoothed a hand across her skin, reveling in the softness. It was like silk, as though his rough hands might snag it and damage its perfection.

"I will miss you, Ian," she whispered, almost too low to be heard.

Ian tensed, as if her words had suddenly stretched him taut. All the reasons he was leaving came rushing back to collide with the exquisite pleasure he had just experienced. He pressed a kiss to her lips, then buried his face in the fragrant hair at her shoulder. "I'll miss you, too."

They held each other in silence for a while, until Mimi stirred. Ian released her and she sat up, scooting away and off the settee. She slipped on her panties, followed quickly by her bra and T-shirt. Aching for her touch, but knowing that she had given more than he could have dreamed, Ian followed her lead. He stepped into his pants, zipped them, but didn't bother with the belt or snap.

Mimi put on her skirt. He watched her run her fingers through her hair, trying to restore order. Ian yearned to do the task for her. He stuck his hands into his pockets to control the urge. Her back was to him for a moment and her shoulders rose on a sigh. When she turned around, she was smiling, but he could see her sorrow. His heart twisted in his chest.

"I came here intending to talk to you about Jack," Mimi said, pushing a lock of hair behind one ear.

"Has he talked to you?"

"About what happened Sunday?" She shook her head. "No. He won't."

"That doesn't give us much to discuss."

"I thought…" Mimi paused and toyed with a parallel ruler on the desk beside her. "I wanted to see if I could get you two together somehow."

"If I leave next week, I don't think that's possible."

She opened her mouth, as if to protest, then closed it again in a frown. "No, I suppose not. He'll like it even less when I tell him you're leaving so soon."

"Has Johnny been around?" he asked, hating to say the name, but realizing he had to know the answer.

She nodded carefully. "They spend time together. Jack likes him."

Ian felt the knife thrust, and a cry of pain rose in his throat. Exactly what he had hoped would happen *was* happening: a father reunited with a son. "That's good," he heard himself say.

"Is it?" Mimi looked at him, a question in her eyes.

"Yes, it is." As much as it hurt, Ian was certain of that fact. "For Jack, it is the best."

"He's going to miss you, too."

"Yeah. He'll get over it."

"Ian, he needs you," Mimi said impatiently.

"Jack needs a *father* more than he needs a friend. You said as much the other night, Mimi."

Biting her lip, Mimi looked at the floor for a moment, then up into his eyes. She took a step, stood before him and put a hand on his cheek. In his pockets, Ian's hands clenched into fists. He wanted to grab her, hold her and never let her go. He restrained the urge. Had this afternoon been a mistake? No. He would never feel that, but he wouldn't compound it either by saying the wrong thing. Mimi's blue eyes were full of something he couldn't grasp. Part sorrow, but there was something else, too.

"Be safe," she said. She kissed him one last time. Seconds later she was gone.

Ian slumped down onto the settee, putting his head in his hands. From the heights of bliss to the depths of despair, all in one hour. Tears stung his eyes and he rubbed them hard. A roll of charts slid off the pile at his feet and onto the floor. He kicked it across the cabin. Then he picked up a bag of rice and chucked that across the cabin, too. It exploded against the bulkhead, grains flying outward and falling to cover everything.

Putting both hands on top of his head, Ian drew in a deep breath, tamping down the incoherent anger. He closed his eyes and counted to ten. When he opened them he dropped his arms and looked around. The boat was a mess. He would have to clean it up and stow everything away properly. The sooner he did, the sooner he could leave. What else could he do? It was time to go.

Chapter Fifteen

Ian slipped into his bunk about four in the morning after picking up the last grain of rice and stowing the last piece of gear. He was tired enough to fall directly into oblivion. As soon as he closed his eyes, though, Mimi came to him and hovered, just out of reach. After lying wide awake for an hour—reliving every taste, every touch of her body—Ian knew that sleep would be hard for many nights to come.

Finally, he dropped off and into a dream about her. She had her guitar and was singing some song that he couldn't quite hear. The melody was haunting, infinitely sad. The dream turned into a nightmare when Johnny showed up and she began to kiss the other man. Helpless to stop it or even scream a protest, Ian awoke with a jerk. He was covered in sweat, the sun high in the morning sky.

Rolling out of bed, he grabbed the clothes he had worn the day before. His head was splitting, pounding as if he had just finished a two-day bender. He popped three aspirin and headed to the shower. Cold water would wash out the cobwebs and get his blood circulating for the day.

The day he was leaving.

Minerva was ready to go. He had provisions as well as spare parts for everything from the engine to the head pump. He would make one last trip to the grocery store for a few fresh vegetables, a block of ice and meats for the cooler. When that was done, he would fill the water tanks. It was eleven now. He would slip the lines by two at the latest and head north up the bay, then through the canal to the Delaware. In two days or less, he could be in the Atlantic, out of sight of land.

AFTER HIS RUN to the grocery store, Ian found his brother, handed him the keys to his truck and bid him farewell.

Patrick hugged him tightly. "Call me when you get to St. Martin. I'll join you for the jump to the ditch."

Ian packed his groceries into *Minerva*'s icebox, then stopped in the office to say goodbye to his mother. She hung up the phone as soon as she saw him.

"Patrick says you're leaving *today*," she said. "Were you going to bother to tell your parents?"

"Of course. I'm leaving, Ma. Bye." Ian waved and turned around.

"Stop right there, young man!"

Ian froze, then smiled at himself ruefully. *Thirty-three and still powerless against his mother's voice.* He turned to face her as she came around the counter. Elaine wore a fierce frown and he expected a severe reprimand. Instead, when she reached him, she put her arms around him in a strong embrace. His arms encircled her just as tightly and he rested his chin on her red curls. They stood like that for a long moment, wordless.

She pulled away, gripping his arms above the elbow as he kept his hands at her waist. "I know you've waited for this a long time. Be safe. Have an adventure, but be safe. I'm so glad you're following your dreams."

She was still frowning and Ian could see she was trying to hide tears. "Ma—"

"We'll come see you after Christmas. Let us know where you're going to be."

Ian smiled and kissed her cheek. "Thanks, Ma. I will."

The door opened and Antonio walked inside. "Here you are. I was just down at *Minerva*. You're set to go?"

"Everything's ready."

"You have charts for Maine?" Antonio asked with a frown. "It was not on your original itinerary. And I don't mean those electronic ones. Never trust those things."

"I'm good to go, Pop. I've got charts, paper and electronic ones both."

"Good." Antonio nodded, then reached out and hugged Ian, as well, pounding him on the back several times. When he drew away, he held Ian's shoulders, shaking him a little. "Be careful. We will miss you."

"Thanks, Pop. I'll miss you, too."

"We'll come help you with the lines," Elaine said.

"I'd rather you didn't." Ian touched her on the arm. "Let's not make a big deal about this, okay?"

Elaine nodded. "Call us when you can. Write when you can't."

"I won't be that far away yet. I'll call when I get to Block Island."

Ian kissed her cheek again and gripped his father's hand. Then he turned and left them. Glancing back over his shoulder, he saw Antonio take Elaine into his arms. They *would* miss him, Elaine especially, but neither of them would ever think of stopping him. In the past, every time he changed his plans—even when his father was ill—they had argued. *Go,* they had said. *Take hold of your dreams.* Ian swallowed down a lump of pride. He couldn't ask for better parents.

When he reached *Minerva*, Ian climbed aboard. He scanned the deck and the rig, mentally checking that each piece of gear was ready. Down below, everything was shipshape and quiet. There was nothing left to do but start the motor. He sat down at the nav desk, strangely hesitant to put the key into the ignition. He thought about his parents again. They always wanted the best for their children, regardless of what it cost them personally. His leaving pained them, but they wouldn't let him see their tears. They only gave encouragement and support.

Ian rubbed a hand across his face. In the same way, his leaving Jack and Mimi hurt him. He would miss them immensely. But he had to believe his departure would be better for them. Jack would discover his father. Maybe Mimi and Johnny could find a way to raise their son together. In both cases, the odds were better if Ian Berzani disappeared for a while.

A pounding of footsteps broke his contemplation. As if conjured from Ian's thoughts, Jack appeared in the companionway. He stood in the sunlight, glaring at Ian. Slowly, Ian stood. "Hey, runt. What's up?"

"You made my mom cry. You're a jerk. A…an *asshole*." The boy spit out the slur defiantly, wielding it as a weapon.

Ian blinked, bewildered. Was he dreaming this? Everything seemed so real. "Hey, wait a minute here. What are you talking about?"

"She cried all night. I heard her. It's your fault!" His eyes dared Ian to deny the accusation.

Ian began to understand. Of course Mimi had cried last night. So had he. Apparently Jack had overheard it and blown it out of proportion. "I didn't mean to. I like your mom."

"You do not. You hate her! You're mean. You made her cry just like you made me cry. I hate you!" With the spill of words, Jack launched himself at Ian from the companionway steps, fists flailing. The attack so surprised Ian that the boy got in two or three blows before Ian caught his wrists and subdued him into a twisting writhe of indignation. "Lemme go!"

"I will. After you calm down," Ian said, keeping Jack tucked close to him.

"I *hate* you," Jack said again, but there were tears in his voice.

"Please, Jack. Don't say that."

But the words spilled out of him, "I hate you, I hate you," again and again, like a volcano of feelings that had no end. He tried to kick and punch. He tried to bite. Anything but listen to reason.

Ian held him tight, whispering, "Calm down, Jack. It's okay," like a soothing mantra. Slowly the boy went limp. Weary and exhausted, he sagged against Ian's grip. As he did, the child began to weep in huge gusts of air. His mouth opened, his eyes scrunched shut in agony.

Ian let go of the thin wrists and picked him up in his arms. Cradling him, Ian sat and rocked the boy back and forth in his lap, instinctively trying to ease the pain. Jack buried his face in Ian's neck as the tears continued to fall, clutching a hand into Ian's shirt. Ian rested his face against Jack's and found himself humming a tuneless reassurance to him.

It occurred to Ian that his father had done the same for him when he was young. More than once, probably, when some unknowable, unfixable feeling had overwhelmed his small soul. Gradually, the tense body relaxed in Ian's arms. The sobs eased; the tremors diminished. After a while, Ian realized Jack had gone to sleep, worn-out from the force of his emotions.

Sitting still, Ian held the boy, unwilling to move. Jack was a warm weight in his arms that felt right. With a shift of position, Ian leaned back into the corner of the settee, stretching his legs out and resting his feet on the opposite seat. His heart ached for Jack's sorrow, but what could he do for him? What would Antonio have done for him? Ian smiled at the comparison. What did a father do, really? Protect, discipline, comfort, provide, guide, cherish. He had done all those things for Jack. It didn't matter that there was no blood between them. It didn't matter that Jack *had* a father. He and Jack had forged a bond that had proved just as valuable and durable as that between any father and son.

Ian gazed down at Jack, asleep, tear-streaked and flushed and very innocent-looking. Brushing the hair away from Jack's eyes, Ian felt a knot inside himself loosen. "I love you, Jack," he said aloud. It seemed like those words were far too long overdue.

Resting his head against the back of the cushions, Ian closed his eyes. Now that he'd admitted his love for this boy—and for his mother—he pondered the next step. Though Mimi hadn't said the words, Ian knew her passion of the day before—and her tears last night—meant that she loved him. In fact, she loved him enough to let him go and follow his dreams. Imagining her in bed alone with her tears, he swallowed. He couldn't allow that any more than he could stand aside and let Jack suffer. Johnny Sinclair be damned! He could not let the man trump his own love for Jack and Mimi.

Jack stirred and Ian opened his eyes. The boy's eyelashes fluttered once, then lifted slowly. He looked up at Ian, bewildered. As memory slowly returned, he struggled to rise and Ian let him slip away. Taking the handkerchief that Ian offered, Jack blew his nose while Ian poured him a glass of water. He handed it to the boy and sat beside him on the settee. Silence stretched between them as Jack drank.

"I'm sorry I made your mom cry," Ian said finally.

Pausing a beat, he added, "I'm sorry I made you cry, too."

Jack shrugged, keeping his eyes on the glass in his hands. He took another sip of water. Ian sighed, unsure of how to go forward. He knew what *he* wanted, but what Jack wanted had yet to be discovered. The boy was giving him no help, either. He tried again. "I've missed you."

"Then how come you didn't come over?" Jack shot a glance at Ian.

"I thought you didn't want to see me. After Sunday." Ian raised a brow and Jack shrugged again. He continued, "And you've had a visitor these past few days, too."

"Johnny Sinclair," Jack said, his eyes lighting up a bit. "He's great."

"Yeah. Pretty cool to have him visit you."

"He's my dad," Jack said matter-of-factly. He set his empty glass on the table while Ian simply stared.

"He told you that?"

"No. No one did."

"You figured that out yourself?"

Jack snorted. "Just because I'm nine doesn't mean I don't know nothing." The boy had an all-too-knowing smirk on his face.

Ian laughed. So much for keeping secrets from the kid. He sobered and looked over at Jack again. "How do you feel about that?"

"I don't know," Jack said, squirming a little. "I mean, he's my dad and all, but he's not my *dad,* y'know?"

"I know." Ian nodded. He put a hand on Jack's shoulder. "Sometimes, you have more than one dad."

Jack nodded as if this was common knowledge. "You're kinda my dad." He glanced at Ian, flushed a little and turned away. But in that second, Ian saw eyes that were very blue and earnest. And hopeful.

Ian's heart swelled. "That's just what I was thinking. So what are we going to do about it?"

Jack thought for a while. "You could marry my mom."

"I've thought about that, too. You wouldn't mind?"

"Uh-uh." He was silent, picking at the welting on the edge of the cushion. "But would you have to go away?" he asked.

"No. I couldn't go away. I'd be the kind of father that stayed right here." Ian squeezed the boy's shoulder. "Unless you and your mom came with me."

The possibility seemed to stun Jack, then he raised his eyes to Ian's again. This time they shone with excitement. "We could do that? Yeah!"

"Maybe someday, but you have to get through school."

Jack frowned, then his face cleared. "I can learn at home, like Stephanie in sailing class. She doesn't go to school. Her mom teaches her and she has homework and everything."

Ian laughed and shook his head. The kid was miles ahead of him. "We'll have to see about that. I don't even know if your mom would want to marry me."

"She would. She likes you a lot."

"You think so?" Jack made it sound so simple. So easy. "I suppose I'd have to ask her."

"I'll go ask her," Jack said, bouncing up.

"Wait a minute, there," Ian said, but Jack was already up the companionway steps.

"Come on!" Jack's voice floated back down into the boat. Ian heard the smack of feet on the dock as the boy jumped off.

Ian scrambled after Jack with a laugh. He had to catch him before he arranged the wedding, honeymoon and the rest of his life. Moments like this could not be rushed.

He caught up with Jack in the parking lot and together they walked toward the Laughing Gull. Ian's long strides just barely kept up with Jack's eager bounds. When Jack's hand found his, Ian felt light and happy.

WHEN ANTONIO AND Elaine Berzani walked into the bar, Mimi was surprised. She had never seen them outside the marina. Then she felt a sharp pain in her heart. Just the sight of them was enough to remind her of Ian. George stepped out from behind the bar to greet them, pulling out a chair for Elaine, kissing her cheek and slapping Antonio on the back.

While they talked, Mimi turned her attention to a glass of cabernet she was pouring. She set it down in front of a woman at the end of the bar and pulled a pint of Guinness for the man sitting next to her. The Gull was busy for this early in the afternoon, regulars already starting to drift in for an end-of-the-week celebration.

George came to the bar, filled a glass with chardonnay and another with ice and a healthy dose of scotch. His face was grim. Mimi came over and touched him on the arm. He picked up two cocktail napkins, not looking at her.

"What's wrong?" she asked.

"He left," George said abruptly. "Today. About an hour ago, Elaine said."

Mimi uttered the only thing that came to mind, her voice thin and far away. "But he said he was leaving next week."

"Antonio said the boat was ready, so he left." George stopped, his jaw working. "No fanfare. He didn't even want his parents to see him off."

Mimi just stared at him. Her brain refused to accept what she had heard.

Her father's eyes met hers. "I'm sorry, Mim."

Closing her eyes tightly, Mimi tried to dam the tears that had been falling off and on since yesterday. One slipped down her cheek before she wiped it away. George hugged her tightly and she clung to him for a long minute. Drawing back, she swallowed and took the napkins he held out to her, pressing them to her eyes.

"I need a minute, Dad." Her voice was clogged with the sorrow she was trying not to let loose.

"Take all the time you need." He stroked a hand over her face. "I wish it had worked out differently."

Mimi pressed her lips together and nodded. Slipping past him, she went out the side door and stood on the patio, staring sightlessly in front of her. A sob fought its way out of her throat. She tried to force it back, but it wrenched from her in a hoarse cry as tears began falling hard and fast. Mimi cursed herself for letting Ian go and at the same time wondered how she could have asked him to stay. She loved him and wanted him to pursue his dreams, just as she had done. She wrapped her arms around herself, offering what comfort she could. It wasn't enough.

"Oh, there you are!" Claire's voice startled Mimi and she jumped. Her mother had come down the path from the house. "Have you seen— Oh, my dear! What's wrong?" Claire drew her daughter into an embrace.

Mimi fell into her arms unhesitatingly. Shaking with sobs, she clung to her mother tightly. "He's gone," she managed to say.

"Who? Jack?"

"No. Ian." Mimi choked and gasped for breath. "I didn't mean to fall in love with him."

"I know, dear. Sometimes love just happens."

The embrace that had soothed her so often as a child was warm and comforting again. Mimi lifted her head from her mother's shoulder and wiped her wet cheeks. Claire gave her a lace-edged handkerchief.

As Mimi tidied herself, Claire gently stroked a hand over her daughter's hair, smoothing it from her brow. "When did you hear about this?"

"Just now. Ian's parents are inside," Mimi said, her voice trembling.

"Oh, you poor dear." She was silent as she studied Mimi's face. Then she glanced around worriedly. "I was looking for Jack. I don't suppose you've seen him?"

Mimi frowned. "Not since I brought him back from school. He went to his room and refused lunch."

"Yes, and when I went upstairs a while ago, he wasn't there. I thought he might have sneaked over here. I'm sorry to bother you with this now."

"No. I'm fine." Mimi steadied herself to face this new problem. "Well, he's not with Ian. We know that much."

"Maybe Elaine or Antonio saw Jack."

Mimi turned and pulled open the door to the bar without another word. Claire followed her inside and they went to the table where the Berzanis sat. There was a round of greetings. Antonio gave Mimi an especially consoling pat on the back. Elaine offered her a comforting hug, too.

Mimi wasn't surprised that Ian's parents knew something had happened between her and their son. The yard—and Crab Creek—was a small place. She simply appreciated their compassion. Tears welled up again, but her concern for Jack trumped her sadness. She began to ask if they had seen her son on their way to the Gull. Before she could finish, the door to the bar burst open and Jack raced inside.

In that instant, Mimi felt equal parts relief that her son was safe and amazement that he appeared to be so happy. Something had changed him. Two seconds later, she—and everyone else around the table—was stunned to see Ian walk through the door.

"Mom! Mom!" Jack rushed up to her and threw his arms around her waist. "Guess what?"

Bewildered by the sight of both of them, Mimi felt faint. The force of Jack's hug alone nearly knocked her over. Mimi knelt and wrapped her arms around Jack, as much to return his embrace, as to regain some equilibrium. "Where have you been?" She looked at his shining face, grinning at her. "Grandmom was worried."

"Mo-*om!* You're not listening to me." Jack wiggled impatiently. "Ian's not leaving!"

Mimi's gaze flew to Ian's, unable to believe what Jack had said. His dark eyes were sending her a message she didn't dare trust, either.

"Are you all right?" Antonio asked his son. "Did something happen?"

Ian grinned. "Yeah. I suppose you could say that."

"He wants to get married to us," Jack said, his hands on Mimi's shoulders. "Can we?"

Mimi felt the world stop, as if someone somewhere had pulled the emergency brake. Gazing up into Ian's eyes, she saw love and longing shining out at her. "I—I…" Was this really happening? Her ears hummed and her heart pounded.

Ian stepped closer to her and pulled her to her feet. "I love you," he said softly, yet with a deep intensity that shook her soul. "And Jack, too. I want us to be a family."

Jack hugged her waist, looking up at them, but it didn't deter Ian from kissing her. In his lips was a promise and a hope for the future. His mouth released hers and he looked into her eyes, asking silently for her answer.

"Oh, please," she gasped. The world suddenly started

to spin again, making her dizzy. Mimi put a hand out and Ian grasped it, steadying her. "Yes. Oh, yes!"

In one swoop, Ian gathered her and Jack into his arms. A wild clamor swelled as all four parents surrounded them. Jack squirmed out of the embrace and ran to hug his grandparents, chattering about all that had happened between him and Ian. Mimi kept her arms tight around Ian's neck, unable to let him go.

"Hey. I'm not going anywhere," he whispered, reading her thoughts. "Not without you and Jack."

She looked up at him. "But what about *Minerva* and your dreams?"

"I've got the dream that matters most right here in my arms."

"Are you sure? I—"

He kissed her quiet. "Dreams are meant to be shared. Will you share mine?"

"Oh, yes. I will." Mimi swallowed down tears. She was not crying anymore today. Not with such happiness all around. "I love you," she said tenderly.

Ian kissed her again, this one long and hard. Voices rose in a cheer and a champagne cork popped. Glasses were raised and Mimi felt her heart soar with love and hope. They would dream together. Forever.

Epilogue

"A glass of wine, my love?" Ian asked.

"Please."

He reached in the cooler for the bottle of white and pulled out a beer for himself. "Jack?" he called. "Water or juice?"

"Juice. Orange." The words drifted down the forward hatch.

"Please?" Mimi said loudly.

"*Puh*-lease."

With a laugh, Ian poured the drinks. "Are we drinking down here or up in the cockpit?"

"Mmm. Cockpit. It's such a nice day. I'll be up there in a minute. I need to get something," Mimi said with a smile.

Ian put down the box of orange juice. "Come here first, Mrs. Berzani."

Pulling her into his arms, he kissed her lightly once, then twice. It wasn't enough, so the third try was deep and lasting. When she pressed up against him, supple and sweet, he stroked his hands down her back to her bottom. He wanted to pick her up and carry her off to bed. Maybe they wouldn't even make it that far. They could replay those memories of making love the first time on the settee. There was a thud on deck and Ian groaned.

"Sometimes having a kid aboard is a pain in the ass," he said against her lips.

Mimi giggled. "There's always tonight."

"I don't want to wait until tonight," he said in a grumble as he released her.

"Then you should have thought of that before you married us."

She sent him a sassy look from under her lashes that did nothing to quench his desire. Ian took a long drink of beer. With a sigh, he gathered up the other two glasses and took them topside. Jack dropped into the cockpit and took the juice.

"This place is awesome! I saw a seal swim right next to the anchor chain."

"So, you think Maine's pretty cool, huh?"

"I wish the water was warmer, but I like it a lot. Can we go kayaking again?"

"Tomorrow. In the afternoon." Ian sipped his beer. "In the morning I have to change the oil on the engine."

"Can I help?"

"I wouldn't dream of doing it without you."

Jack grinned and drank his juice down thirstily. Ian smiled and sat back, propping his feet on the bench beside his son. His stepson, actually, but as far as he and Jack were concerned, there was no "step" between them. Johnny saw Jack whenever his touring permitted, but neither he nor Jack wanted anything more than an intermittent friendship. Johnny wasn't cut out for the role of father, at least not right now. He sent albums, T-shirts and the occasional free concert tickets. Jack was content with that and proud to claim Ian as his real father.

Johnny's latest release was a song written by none other than Mimi Green. He had found some of her music in an old guitar case—the real reason he had returned to see her and Jack in the first place. Before he left for a tour of the West Coast, he had asked her if he could record three of them. Inspired, Mimi had written more songs, one of which Johnny had passed on to another band.

From that success, Mimi had gotten other requests for songwriting. She had even collaborated with a couple of bands on new music for their albums. Singing was part of her life again, too. She performed regularly whenever she could. Luckily her dream was as portable as Ian's.

They were living part of his dream by sailing in Maine for the summer. Together with Jack, they had rebuilt their lives and hopes for the future into a happy present. Ian had never thought he could be so content. He wasn't sailing around the globe, but he found that his small corner of the world with Mimi and Jack held adventure enough.

A box wrapped in bright red, star-studded paper appeared in the companionway. Mimi followed it, a wide grin on her face. Ian dropped his feet and sat up as she pushed the box toward him.

"Happy Birthday!"

"I thought we were gonna give him his presents later," Jack said, frowning and bouncing up and down on his seat at the same time. "After cake."

"I couldn't wait," Mimi said, laughing. "Besides, this is a gift for all of us."

Ian rested the heavy box in his lap so that she could sit next to him. He handed her the glass of wine with a kiss. "You shouldn't have."

"But I did," she said, smiling and giving him a steamy look that set his pulse pounding.

"Come on, guys. No more kissy stuff," Jack said, rolling his eyes. "Open the present."

Ian pulled the bow off and carefully separated the tape

and paper at one end, doing it slowly because he knew how the anticipation drove Jack crazy.

"Hurry up!" the boy begged.

Finally, the paper came off in one piece. With his rigging knife, Ian slit the tape along the top of the cardboard box. Inside, he saw what looked like schoolbooks. Taking one out, he flipped through it. "You think I need remedial education?" he asked Mimi.

"Books? How boring." Jack peered over the edge of the box. "Is that all?"

Mimi laughed at both of them. "They may be boring, but you'd better study them well. I give hard tests."

"Huh?"

Ian was just as confused as his son. "What are you up to?"

"It's Jack's homeschooling program. The first semester."

Ian looked at her blankly, not following where she was going with this.

"I'm sure sailing around the world will be instructive, but Jack needs a traditional, well-rounded program, too." She cocked her head and gave him a narrow-eyed, stern look. "But we're *both* going to be his teachers. I'm not doing it alone."

Understanding flickered in Ian's head. "Mimi, are you sure? This isn't what we planned."

She covered his mouth with her fingers. "A wise man once told me that dreams are meant to be shared. If you want to sail around the world, then I do, too." She shot a look at Jack, who was still confused. "What do you think? Are you willing to give up regular school for a bit of sailing?"

Jack whooped in joy as Ian pulled his wife into a hard

embrace. "Thank you," he whispered in her ear. "I love you."

Her answer was lost in the pounding of his heart and buried under his lips as he kissed her. He didn't need to hear the words, though. The box in his lap said everything. A new dream was beginning, forged out of their hearts. He couldn't wait to get started.

Neither could Jack.

* * * * *

Look for Lisa Ruff's
next book BABY BOMBSHELL *and watch*
the sparks fly between
Evan McKenzie and
Anna Berzani!
Available in August 2010,
wherever Harlequin
books are sold.

*Harlequin Intrigue top author Delores Fossen presents
a brand-new series of breathtaking romantic suspense!*
TEXAS MATERNITY: HOSTAGES
The first installment available May 2010:
THE BABY'S GUARDIAN

Shaw cursed and hooked his arm around Sabrina.

Despite the urgency that the deadly gunfire created, he tried to be careful with her, and he took the brunt of the fall when he pulled her to the ground. His shoulder hit hard, but he held on tight to his gun so that it wouldn't be jarred from his hand.

Shaw didn't stop there. He crawled over Sabrina, sheltering her pregnant belly with his body, and he came up ready to return fire.

This was obviously a situation he'd wanted to avoid at all cost. He didn't want his baby in the middle of a fight with these armed fugitives, but when they fired that shot, they'd left him no choice. Now, the trick was to get Sabrina safely out of there.

"Get down," someone on the SWAT team yelled from the roof of the adjacent building.

Shaw did. He dropped lower, covering Sabrina as best he could.

There was another shot, but this one came from a rifleman on the SWAT team. Shaw didn't look up, but he heard the sound of glass being blown apart.

The shots continued, all coming from his men, which meant it might be time to try to get Sabrina to better cover. Shaw glanced at the front of the building.

So that Sabrina's pregnant belly wouldn't be smashed against the ground, Shaw eased off her and moved her to a sitting position so that her back was against the brick wall. They were close. Too close. And face-to-face.

He found himself staring right into those sea-green eyes.

How will Shaw get Sabrina out?
Follow the daring rescue and the heartbreaking
aftermath in THE BABY'S GUARDIAN
by Delores Fossen,
available May 2010 from Harlequin Intrigue.

HARLEQUIN® *Blaze*™

is proud to introduce...

New York Times bestselling author

Brenda Jackson

with
SPONTANEOUS

Kim Cannon and Duan Jeffries have a great thing going.
Whenever they meet up, the passion between them
is hot, intense…spontaneous. And things really heat
up when Duan agrees to accompany her to her
mother's wedding. Too bad there's something
he's not telling her….

Don't miss the fireworks!

*Available in May 2010
wherever Harlequin Blaze books are sold.*

---

red-hot reads

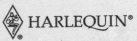

HARLEQUIN®

LAURA MARIE ALTOM

The Baby Twins

Stephanie Olmstead has her hands full raising
her twin baby girls on her own. When she runs
into old friend Brady Flynn, she's shocked to find
herself suddenly attracted to the handsome airline
pilot! Will this flyboy be the perfect daddy—
or will he crash and burn?

Babies
&
Bachelors
USA

"LOVE, HOME & HAPPINESS"

www.eHarlequin.com

HAR75309

Former bad boy Sloan Hawkins is back in
Redemption, Oklahoma, to help keep his aunt's
cherished garden thriving and to reconnect with the
girl he left behind, Annie Markham. But when he
discovers his secret child—and that single mother
Annie never stopped loving him—he's determined
that a wedding will take place in the garden
nurtured by faith and love.

Where healing flows...

Look for
The Wedding Garden
by Linda Goodnight

Available May 2010
wherever you buy books.

Steeple
Hill®
LI87595

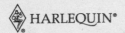

HARLEQUIN®

Showcase

On sale May 11, 2010

Reader favorites from the most talented voices in romance

Save $1.00 on the purchase of 1 or more Harlequin® Showcase books.

SAVE $1.00

on the purchase of 1 or more Harlequin® Showcase books.

Coupon expires Oct 31, 2010. Redeemable at participating retail outlets. Limit one coupon per purchase. Valid in the U.S.A. and Canada only.

52609015

5 65373 00076 2   (8100)0 11651

HSCCOUP0410

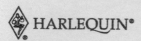
HARLEQUIN®

American ★ Romance®

COMING NEXT MONTH

Available May 11, 2010

#1305 THE BABY TWINS
Babies & Bachelors USA
Laura Marie Altom

#1306 THE MAVERICK
Texas Outlaws
Jan Hudson

#1307 THE ACCIDENTAL SHERIFF
Fatherhood
Cathy McDavid

#1308 DREAM DADDY
Daly Thompson

www.eHarlequin.com